Carmen Street
Maggie's Story

April Gutierrez

Author Website:
www.aprilgutierrez.com

Editing by: Karen Venancio of Brooksville, FL
Contact: KVee014@gmail.com

ISBN: 069246266X
ISBN-13: 9780692462669

DEDICATION

To old childhood friends that gave me family, freedom and
love never to be forgotten.

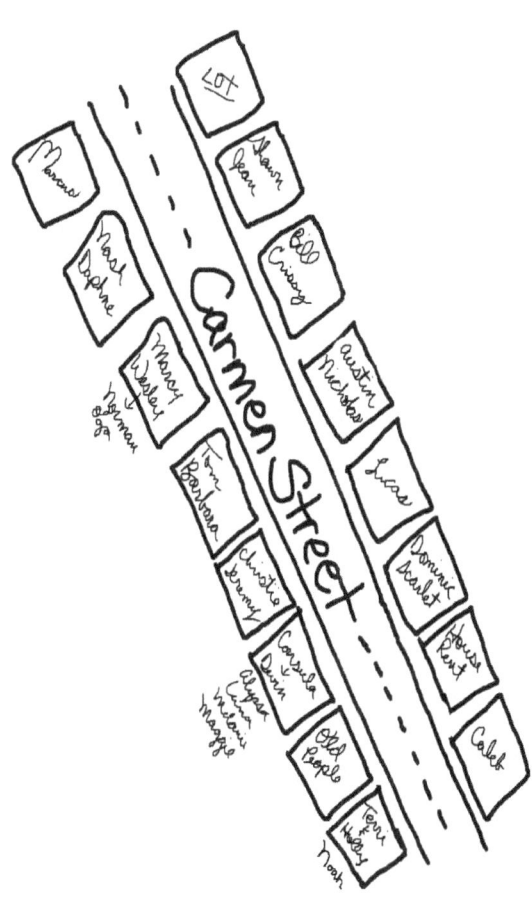

ACKNOWLEDGMENTS

History has shown me that a story from our past can be altered by anyone who holds the memory. Fictional stories are always lined with some truths. Maggie's story is lined with a truth of how it was for everyone growing up on Carmen Street in the 80's and 90's. The memories are not just with one but with twenty neighborhood kids who became friends.

In a time where parents didn't fear their children being physically harmed by the sick and twisted, we played from sunrise to sunset. Our friendships were not a whim on the breeze of a decade but of a lifetime that has yet to snap.

1 COMING HOME

June 2015

Driving down Carmen Street was something Maggie never thought she would do again. Actually, it was something she promised herself, ten years ago, she would never do. Go back to the one place that caused her so much pain. Yet, there she was, making the familiar turn off of Himes down the street she grew up on. The houses, while a little older still looked the same. It was the trees that proved how much time had passed. The trees she'd climbed as a child and hid behind during so many games of man hunt with her friends, is the telling detail of time lost.

"You okay?" her brother, Devin asked her, while turning into her grandmother's driveway.

She nodded but didn't make eye contact with him. "I'm fine," she sighed.

"Abuelita is so excited that you are here."

Maggie looked to her brother, the genuine appreciation tugged at her heart. "It's been a long time since I was here."

He unbuckled his seatbelt. "I'm sure she will make a few comments about that," he teased.

"Yeah, well, I have a busy schedule."

"We know, Margaret. I'm just saying, she will be thrilled to hold you and be able to have a conversation with you in real life. It's not the same as talking to you via Skype."

Maggie nodded, not disagreeing with her brother.

Devin got out of the car, leaving her there to think for a moment. She heard the trunk open, realizing that he was taking out her luggage. Much like the doorman did back at home in Chicago.

"What am I doing here?" she whispered to herself.

A part of her didn't want to look out the window to the neighboring houses because she knew that it would bring in too many unwanted memories.

"Are you coming?" he asked her through the front windshield.

That was it, the point of no return. She opened the car door and felt the Florida heat hitting her cheeks. The flood of sunlight, spreading across her skin, felt like a warm blanket.

"Oh, how I've missed the warmth," she sighed, eyes closed, with her face to the sun.

"I bet," he laughed, walking to the front door.

But the moment she opened her eyes, she noticed the one house she hadn't wanted to see. The front window shutters looked a little shabby, which mirrored the way the mailbox stood as though it was sad on a summer's day. She heard her brother clear his throat and her head snapped to Devin. She decided she would have to find a way to push past the memories.

"Come on," he called to her at the door, her things already inside.

Devin held the door opened for his sister as she made her way inside the house. He watched as the emotions raced through her, she'd always been an open book to him. He'd known his sister had dealt with a lot, ten years ago, before she left town. He'd seen her rollercoaster relationship with Nicholas first hand, and how it ended abruptly. While he'd never talked to her about it openly, he knew what had happened and why she would never want to come home again.

"Is that my Niña walking through the door?" Consuela asked, the excitement in her voice evident.

"Si Abuelita, it's me," Maggie smiled, meeting her grandmother in the hallway. If a hug could tell a story, that story would be of pure bliss.

Consuela has many grandchildren, all of which she loves deeply, but her greatest joy was when Margaret was born. Something about that tiny little miracle stole her heart the moment she met her.

"It has been too long," Consuela whispered in her granddaughter's ear.

"I'm sorry I couldn't make it before now," Margaret sighed, a single tear welling up in her eye.

"Bueno," Consuela stiffly said as she pulled away, taking in the sight of her now 28 year old granddaughter. "You are too thin. I have made you some lunch, your favorite."

Maggie's eyes widened. "You didn't," she giggled in anticipation.

"The poor man's mean no more, Mi-ha."

Consuela was referring to a Cuban classic lunch: White rice, fried eggs, and platanos, otherwise known as plantains.

"My platanitos never turns out like yours Abuelita. Something just doesn't add up," Maggie admitted sheepishly.

"It must be the love that's missing," Devin interrupted, coming into the kitchen from the hallway.

Margaret smiled at her brother, knowing it was something that had always been said about their grandmother's cooking. Her love was what made everything seem to taste so much richer.

"Yes, that and common cooking sense," Consuela teased.

The three of them sat at the kitchen table and ate as if time hadn't passed.

"When is the funeral?" Maggie asked quietly. The somber reality of her visit waking them out of the past.

"Barbara said it would start at 11:00 tomorrow morning. I'm going to go over there later to see if she needs me to help her with anything," Consuela said, before taking the last bite of her lunch.

"I was hoping to rest for a little while but I could go over there with you if you want," Maggie offered.

Consuela smiled at her granddaughter and thought of what it must feel like to return home after so much time away.

"Your mother would be so proud of you, Margaret."

She shook her head, not wanting to think of her parents yet. "I'm not perfect, Abuelita."

Devin let out a loud huff, "as if being a successful author isn't enough. Look at me, I'm still stuck at the same company since you left."

"That is just nonsense Devin. You are a regional supervisor of a big accounting firm. You are successful, too!"

"Mira, the two of you have a lot to be thankful for, and your parents would be proud of both of you," Consuela tried to soothe out any tension between the siblings.

Devin smiled to himself as he finished his lunch and Maggie took notice.

"Where is Mary?" she asked him, curious how his wife was doing. Mary and Devin had come to Chicago to visit her two years ago when Maggie had released her 7th novel. They looked content, but their relationship seemed distant.

"She is at work. She said she would see you soon. I'm sure she is going to stop by, we usually keep Abuelita company here and have dinner together."

Maggie's attention shot over to her grandmother who had gotten up and began to clean up the dishes. "Abuelita, let me do that. You should be resting."

As if insulted, Consuela turned around and shot her granddaughter a glare, "I may be old but I am not an 'invalida'."

Her use of Spanish words combined with her English was amusing. She defined the use of Spanglish as part of normal Tampa living.

"No one is calling you an invalida, Abuelita. I'm just saying that we can help you," Maggie replied, trying not to sass her grandmother, as clearly she was wanting to.

"Are you kidding me, she lets me do more around the house since her fall."

"Her fall?" Maggie shot out quickly.

Consuela eyeballed her grandson, mentally scolding him for bringing it up. If there was one thing Consuela didn't like was others knowing when she was vulnerable.

"Nada, don't worry about it. I fell and bumped my head a little. I'm fine. He is making more of it than anyone else."

Maggie got up from her seat and motioned from Devin to Consuela. "What do you mean, than anyone else?"

"I took her to the doctors to make sure that she was fine. They didn't see anything but said that she has osteoporosis and needs to be careful because another fall like that could lead to broken bones."

"That is not 'nothing'!" Maggie scolded her grandmother. The pain in her eyes signaled to Consuela that her concern was rooted to a past without her parents. She knew that her grand-daughter's imagination was connecting a future without her in it.

"I'm fine. I will be fine, and look, I even bought myself a new pair of shoes. They have gripping soles to prevent such a fall from happening again," Consuela motioned to her new shoes.

Maggie wasn't sold and the worry filled her more than she had wanted to admit. She was only 10 years old when her parents had died in an accident. That's when she'd gone to live with her grandmother on Carmen Street. Devin was almost out of high school when the accident happened, just barely an adult himself. Before that moment, Maggie hadn't spent too much time at her grandmother's house. She'd heard stories of the neighborhood, and the kids who lived there, but she was still too young to play with them and know anything about them.

At ten years old she'd lost her parents and the only family she'd ever known. But the moment she moved to Carmen Street, Maggie became a part of a different type of family, an unconventional sort.

2 IF HISTORY SERVES ME RIGHT
Maggie

March 1996

The cemetery was filled with strangers. I'd always known that mom and dad had a lot of friends but I'd never imagined to see this many people here.

Devin hasn't taken off his sunglasses since we got out of the car. He stood next to me like a statue, unmoving and emotionless. Staring forward to the priest giving the service, it was like I was standing alone amongst hundreds.

I'd cried so much in the past few days, today it felt like the well had dried up. Although everyone around me carried a handkerchief and somber expressions, I stood, wide eyed and wondering.

Was this all there would be? No more happy thoughts, no more happy memories?

At some point, Abuelita took my hand and walked me over to a headstone off in the distance from where my mother and father now rested.

"Margaret, Nina, I too lost my family once, and I felt like nothing would ever be bright again, and then I met your Abuelo. He was my best friend, the love of my life. He reminded me that while we may lose our path and anchors in life, we can choose to find our way back into the light of life."

I squeezed her hand, I hadn't lost my anchor. She was standing next to me, doing her best to make me understand that while I may now be an orphan, I wasn't alone.

We'd gone back to my parent's house that night and packed my bags. My soul was numb, and I knew it somehow. I'd closed my eyes, and could still see momma's face, smiling at me but how long was that going to last? How long would I remember her face, her voice?

Devin had asked me if I wanted him to stay with me at Abuelita's for a while. I didn't know what to say, but I knew he was asking as much for himself as he was asking for my benefit.

"Yes," I'd replied, as I finished putting stuffed animals in a black bag.

"You are going to like it at Abuela's. The neighborhood kids are nice."

I didn't connect the dots about the neighborhood kids because I'd only been at her house on holidays and never went outside to play.

It wasn't until the following day that I realized what he meant.

Spring break + Sunny Florida weather = stick ball tournament during the day and a neighborhood wide manhunt when the sun settled behind the horizon.

At noon, I found myself sitting on a metal chair in the front porch area of Abuelita's house. My focus was on my cousins who'd been dropped off earlier that morning. The girls stood in line waiting to have their shot at shaming the boys in this round of the game. They played without a care in the world.

My oldest cousin, Luna was first in line to bat. Her boyfriend, Caleb was the pitcher for the opposing team.

"Come on, babe. I'm going to throw it right to you this time. Hit it with all you've got," he encouraged her.

I'd heard the last time he'd said that to her his aim was way off. She'd ended up striking out but she'd popped him a kiss anyway. This time was different, I thought. She was moving herself and had her eye on the ball. When he let go of the ball, he proved to be playing nice but she had no intention of missing again. She struck it with a force, sending it out and far towards the end of the street. No one was out that far and Luna managed to get a homerun. The rest of the girls cheered for her as she brought it in for the score.

Luna, exhausted by the play walked up to the house and took the empty seat next to me, her sight still set on the game.

I focused on her. My cousin, someone who I'd spent maybe 2% of my life around. Everything about her was beautiful. Maybe I thought that solely because I idolized her, the type of girl I wanted to grow up to be. Popular and physically attractive.

"You want to play, Maggie?" she asked me when she realized I was staring at her.

I shook my head at her and turned to look out at the game.

"I'm sure you'd have a lot of fun," Luna tried.

My head shook again. The words stifled by the shyness I was overcome by. I didn't know any of those kids and yet they were so very familiar.

"Well, if you change your mind, you can come stand by me." She smiled and left my side, glancing back once as she got herself out into the road, her team now on defense.

Devin was playing on the boy's team. When he came up to bat, he quickly struck out. He'd stood back in line to bat again until he looked over to me.

"Maggie, come play with us," he yelled to me from across the front yard.

"I'm good," I yelled back at him, now embarrassed by the attention that I was getting.

"Don't be such a little girl, come play with us."

"I am a little girl!" I scolded, feeling the heat rise to my cheeks.

Looking out at the boys in line, I made eye contact with one of them. He wasn't my age, but he wasn't as old as Devin either. He held my glare for a moment before turning to watch the game. His wavy brown hair catching in the wind caused a tingle in my stomach.

I watched him the rest of the game. He'd become my focal point for the afternoon. Every now and again I would catch him look my way, his dazzling green eyes peering into mine. He would hold my eye for a moment, almost as if he were telling me a secret, and then he would go back to what he was doing.

When the game was over, my cousin Melanie ran over to my side.

"Oh, my goodness Maggie. You can't be so lame. You have to come play with us," she sassed.

Melanie is my age but you wouldn't guess by her immaturity. "Why did you spend your whole morning just watching?"

"I don't know how to play stickball, Mel," I replied drily.

"Then you need to ask Devin to teach you because this is all they ever do around here."

It was good to know, but how would I ask my almost adult brother to teach me to do something when he could hardly stand to be around me.

"Maybe later," I told Melanie and I'd only said it to get her to leave me alone about stick ball, already.

Still sitting on the porch, I watched as Luna wrapped her arms around Caleb and kissed him. They looked so in love. I wondered if they would get married. Does that sort of thing happen?

"Do all these kids live on the block?" I asked Melanie, who was sitting in the seat next to me.

"Well, not all of them. Some of them live within a few blocks from here. They all know each other from school."

"We don't go to school with any of them," I said plainly.

"No, see the bigger kids around Devin. They all go to Jefferson, the high school. I mean, I think they are all in the same grade but I'm not sure." She pointed to another set of kids, "those kids go to Wilson, the junior high school. They will go to Jefferson next year I'm sure."

"And everyone just hangs out together no matter what the age difference is?"

"Well, Dominic's sister Scarlet is always hanging around so he doesn't mind. Same thing with Marcy's little brother, Wesley. Devin hangs out with Austin and his younger brother, Nicholas, is always with them. No one really seems to care."

"We are the youngest aren't we?" I asked her solemnly, my face scrunching at her.

She nodded her head at me, "I'm afraid so."

"But look at it this way, at least we can still hang out with them and they are always playing outside at night. Abuelita doesn't mind as long as we are inside at dinner time."

I looked over to the kids hanging out and talking with each other before the start of their next game.

"At least come sit out there with me so you can officially meet everyone."

I didn't know how to summon the courage needed at ten years old to submerse myself into a new group of people.

If history serves me right, they were towering giants who laughed at each other's jokes and teased to a fault. They were family to one another, and not just because most of them were siblings, no, they were family because they had each other in all things.

I let Melanie walk me out that afternoon to participate in the next game of stick ball and believe me when I say I was terrible at it. I knew I sucked at the game, and probably no one would ever want me on their team, but it didn't bother me.

Why? Because every one of those kids cheered me on. They knew what I was going through because Devin was going through it too and they didn't want me to hurt. They patted my back as I stuck out and said, 'maybe next time'. While I couldn't see how next time would get any better, they could. They'd been 10 once, I trusted their encouragement because that's what family does.

3 TWO HOUSES DOWN

June 2015

Consuela had known Tom and Barbara for most of her life. Their children grew up together, the first set of neighborhood kids to grow up on Carmen Street. Their children fell in love and got married. While Tom's death was no big surprise, it still struck home.

"You know, I never did ask you if you have a will, Abuelita," Maggie asked.

"Mi-ha, don't tell me you are going to start in like your brother," she sassed Maggie, as she picked up a blanket from the sofa and absentmindedly folded it.

Maggie could only imagine how Devin was bothering her about such things. He is in fact a monies man. His business back ground puts him in a literal form of mind. Always looking to the future. Always planning for what might happen.

"I just don't want to see your wishes ignored is all," she suggested, while her hands rose in a defensive manner.

"I wish for you to get up off your culo and walk me to Barbara's," she smacked Maggie's leg as she walked out of the living room.

Maggie hadn't seen Barbara since she'd left Florida. Her father's mother was one of the main reasons for her swift departure ten years ago. Not that many knew of course, but her lack of support at the time and overzealous judgments pushed Maggie to the furthest place she could run.

"Are you coming?" Consuela asked, now annoyed Maggie was still sitting pretty on the sofa.

Getting up, her eye caught the house in view from the living room window. She wondered if Nicholas would come to her grandfather's funeral. His childhood home looked empty, void of so much life it once held.

"Wait up!" Maggie yelled as she heard the kitchen door open and slam shut.

Maggie caught up with her grandmother, she hadn't gotten far out the door and into the drive way.

"Sorry," she apologized.

Consuela looked over to her grand-daughter and huffed. "You don't think I know why you hesitate?"

It wouldn't take much to put two and two together to figure out why Maggie had stayed away for such a long time, and yet, no one had bothered to ask. Not once.

"It doesn't matter anymore," Maggie sighed as she walked out in plain sight for everyone to see her, if anyone was looking that is to say.

"You're right, it probably doesn't matter anymore, but then again, you can still see your grandmother. You can still hold her and repent for the sadness you may have caused her. The same cannot be said about your grandfather." She spoke quietly, "may he rest in peace."

Maggie nodded because Consuela was right. She was here to make amends for the pain she'd caused so many years ago. She wasn't here to sulk in the pain she'd felt when she left. All that sadness was behind her. At least, that is what she kept telling herself.

"Have you spoken to anyone since you left?" she'd asked her granddaughter as she half heartedly glanced over to Nicholas' parent's house.

"Not really. Devin tries to tell me things, but I find a way to change the subject before I hear any of it."

"Was it so painful?" she stopped walking all together, her hand reaching out to Maggie's forearm.

"Like you said, Abuelita, it doesn't matter anymore. I know I should have come home. I should have talked to them, make amends for all the horrible things I said and did, but the silence became too much. The wall was built too thick."

"You will find, that a mere smile can tumble those walls in a heartbeat."

"Yes, and one would have to be face to face to feel that sort of triumph."

Consuela understood her granddaughter. Only one can hope Barbara owns up to her end of the deal they'd made on Tom's death bed.

"Come on, your grandmother is expecting us," She said, nudging Maggie along.

The front porch light was on, a beacon of hope, like calling loved ones in for the evening.

The old woman walked to the front screen door just as they walked up the porch steps. Maggie felt hope, a hope she'd long forgotten. The woman looked so much the same, and yet, she was different. The bitterness had faded from the creases on her face. Her eyes light up, they did not show scorn or hatred.

"My girl!" she gasped and covered her mouth with her wrinkled hands. Maggie recalled the nickname from her childhood.

Consuela pulled open the screen door and Maggie reached out to her other grandmother. Their hug made all anguish seem distant. A happy reunion was something bright and beautiful in a time of sadness and loss.

"You are so beautiful!" Barbara whispered into Maggie's ear as she caressed the back of her long dark hair.

A joyful tear gently filled Maggie's eye and threatened to spill but never managed to leave its place. The blurred vision momentarily playing with her sight.

She'd thought she had seen a figure towards the back of the house, but looking clearer proved she'd been mistaken.

"Are you okay, my dear? You've tensed up," Barbara managed as they pulled away from one another.

"I'm fine. How are you?" Maggie changed the subject, making small talk as they all situated themselves on the living room sofas.

"Oh, you know, making the best of it. Your grandfather was ill for such a long time. He is in a better place now. No longer in any pain." Barbara looked from Maggie to Consuela.

Consuela got up, "Can I get us some tea?" she offered the two of them, as if it were her house and it was only natural to be their host." Maggie raised an eyebrow at her.

"Always such the pleaser Abuelita?" Maggie teased, not wanting her to overdo it.

"I can't sit still child, you should know that by now."

Barbara nodded to Consuela and turned back to Maggie. "And what about you? We heard one of your books is getting made into a movie. Isn't that thrilling?"

Maggie never liked talking about her work, mostly because she felt it seemed like boasting, or bragging, but the truth of her current news was rather exciting.

"It really is something. I never could have imagined that someone would want to make one of them into a movie," Maggie smiled at her grandmother.

"Well, Tom and I both went to the bookstore down the road when your last book was released. We were one of the first customers in line to get it. He was so proud of you."

"It's nice to hear," Maggie smiled, not knowing how else to react to hearing that her grandfather was proud of her. Especially when they hadn't even discussed the water under the bridge.

"Mira, I'm just going to come out and say it, Margaret..." Consuela started as she walked back in the living room caring a tray with three tall glasses. "Your grandfather was upset for a few years, but when he saw that you had made something of yourself, he felt that what happened, happened for a reason."

Maggie sat shocked. Not knowing how else to respond other than to take a gulp of tea and listen to what they needed to get off their chest.

"I was wrong for calling you all those horrible names. You were 18 and could do what you damn well pleased with your life and your body, but we grew up with different rules and values in life. We thought we had helped raise you with those values," Barbara shook her head at herself.

"We didn't know at the time how wrong we were being with our judgments. We never imagined you would react in the manner in which you did. Regret had, in fact, filled his heart and he wanted you to know how much he loved you, before he died. We promised him we would tell you that he forgave you and that he hoped you would forgive him too."

Maggie listened to her grandmother speak. She recalled the argument that had transpired between the three of them. She picked up on the words regret and promise but failed to see the point.

This was the current problem that Maggie faced on a day to day basis. Somewhere along the line, she'd become desensitized to the situation that forced her to leave. She had to go or everything beautiful that had filled her life would be tainted, and she refused to let that happen.

"Everything is fine now, Grandma," she said to Barbara. The words were empty, the emotion gone. It was as if she had practiced saying those 5 words so much that when she would finally need to say them, it wouldn't be laced with the feelings, the emotional baggage that was once involved.

"Well then, "Consuela added, looking awkwardly from Maggie to Barbara, "What did you say you needed my help with?"

If one thing was certain, it was that Maggie learned how to change the topic of conversation from the pro herself. Consuela managed to get Barbara out of the past and back to the present. It was something Maggie had planned on doing the whole visit.

The only tremor she felt was when the need took over and she found herself looking out the window to stare at his house.

Old habits are hard to break.

4 WAITING
Maggie

I'd found myself in a pattern, a horrible, terrible, obsessive pattern. Every day, I would come home from school and wait for him.

The neighborhood kids spent less time together during the week being that everyone was on different schedules. The weekends were a different story however, we still spent them together and family hadn't left the circle yet.

But during the week, it was only 4 of us. Melanie and I, still being in middle school, got home before the high school kids let out. We would wait for Nicholas and Wesley to get home so we could play basketball together, or whatever they wanted to do, actually.

It was a ploy....always a ploy. Life at school was terrible and I'd begged Abuelita to transfer me to a different middle school but she refused to see my reasoning. My only escape were my real friends....my family outside of family, the neighborhood that finally made me whole.

While Melanie would sit at the kitchen table to do homework, I would sit across from her and act as though my disinterest was because math was just not my subject. Truth of the matter was that I was staring at his driveway through the window in the kitchen.

The worst part was feeling like the waiting would drag on forever and they would never come home. More often than not, I would take a bike ride alone, around the neighborhood, until magically their vehicles were in the driveway.

Have you ever seen a puppy dog as their owner gets home? It's a visual I hadn't wanted to compare myself to at 13 years old, but nothing more could have hit the nail on the head as to my reaction seeing those two boys getting home.

When Melanie joined me in the 'waiting' and we saw the boys come home, we'd run from our seats, either inside the house or on the front porch, to stand before them, trying to act as mature and adult like as possible.

Fine, we were boy crazy, attention seekers and moreover needy little things, but at 13, they didn't see us as anything else but the little sisters of their friends and that was perfectly fine with us. For Christ's sakes, we were still playing with Barbie dolls at that age.

But the waiting...that is something I will never forget. The feeling that if I wasn't watching as his truck pulled into the driveway, I was going to miss a spectacular event. Like a shooting star, or a golden hued sun, setting for the first time, after weeks of rain.

At that age, I wondered a lot about relationships. There was this one afternoon, a day that will stay with me forever. Probably because it was the day I realized our neighborhood had a history for romance and terrible heartbreak.

Devin was already working part time and taking college classes at the community college in town. I spent most of my time with Melanie, and knew that I would see my brother on the weekends.

He was not in a serious relationship, so I basically only saw him during the day on Saturday because he frequented Ybor City every Saturday night. It was the happening place to be, the club strip near downtown Tampa. On Sundays, I was lucky if I saw him awake before dinner.

I'd known all my life that mom and dad had grown up together on the block. I'd seen Luna and Caleb kissing and hugging all over each other while we hung out since I was 10, but the backlash of neighborhood first love was when the girl didn't get the guy.

The downside of spending so much time with these kids was the emotional rollercoaster you'd signed yourself up for, unknowingly. Spend enough time with a person and you feel something for them. Whether the emotions were real, fake, or completely ridiculous was beside the point. Our perception of emotion is what drives our desire.

This one day, Devin asked me to sit and take score of their stick ball game and something told me it had everything to do with a girl and nothing to do with fairness.

"Watch what you're doing man!" Devin yelled at Dominic for pitching the ball too close to him at the faux pitcher's mound.

"Stop being such a baby," Dominic sassed back, laughing with his teammates at the almost body hit.

"Don't worry about it Dev! Just keep your eye on the ball!" Scarlet encouraged, as any teammate would do….the only standout mention to the interaction was that Scarlet was not part of Dev's team.

There it was, something I'd missed, something I'd not been told. Devin and Scarlet made eyes at one another once he made it to 1st base. There was a spark in their connection, an endearment.

I looked to Nicholas who was enthralled in the game and genuinely wondered if I looked at him like that?

I did…so much so that I looked for that connection between many of the pairs in our group of friends to see if what I felt had any foundation.

Jeremy, next door, spent a little too much time with my

cousin, Alyssa. Though no one would think so because they were never seen together, alone. I could tell in where they placed themselves. If we were all in one person's yard, leaning up against or sitting on cars, Jeremy and Alyssa were always next to each other. I took notice of everyone's interactions after that game.

After my bedtime, when Devin would sit out on the porch with his friends, I'd tiptoe to the windows in the living room and listened, in the dark, to their private conversations.

In that same month, after weeks of snooping in the dark hours, I finally heard why Dominic was upset with Devin.

"He just doesn't understand, Dev," Scarlet said to my brother.

"He is your brother, he isn't supposed to understand. I swear if Maggie felt like I do, I would knock out whoever it was that was making her feel this need."

I peeked out the window at the shocking admission he'd made to Scarlet.

"You need me?" I heard her say, the look on her face a mixture of anguish and of pure joy.

He shook his head, looking down to his hands as they lay on his legs which were stretched out on the lawn chair, "Yeah, I do."

"He's my brother, Dev. He is your best friend. I can't choose between the two of you," she said, placing her head on his shoulder.

"I'm not asking you to choose," he sighed, "I just wish he would accept it and let things be."

She giggled, "it might be because he does know you too well."

Devin laughed and put his arm around her shoulder, "Yeah, but I'm not like that with you and he knows that. We've grown up together, I can't brush you off the way I've done with other girls."

"You better not," she sighed, but I could hear the warning in her voice.

"Think about it, Scarlet. Our families have been friends for decades. I would be pretty stupid to go hurting the neighborhood sweetheart."

They sat there, Scarlet wrapped in Devin's embrace long enough for my eyelids to get heavy. I didn't even realize falling asleep under the window, or being picked up and taken to my bed, but I woke up the next morning with my brother sitting on the corner of my bed staring out the window to our back yard.

"Good morning," I whispered to him.

"Good morning," he replied, his attention still out the window.

"Did you bring me to bed?"

"What are you doing, Maggie?" he asked curtly, bringing down his head to face me square on.

"What do you mean?"

"What do I mean?" his whole body seemed to change, his demeanor tense.

"I don't understand," I clarified, now completely awake.

"You are now old enough to realize when you are being rude and when to mind your own business."

"I didn't mean it like that," I tried to interrupt but he raised his hand at me.

"Let me finish."

His head dropped and I could tell he was troubled. That was when I found myself sitting up and reaching out to him. I wrapped my arms around him and gave him a hug.

"I don't know how to be the type of man you need in your life," he said softly into my hair, his arms slowly wrapping around my tiny figure.

"All I need is a brother, Devin. I'm sorry I eavesdropped on your conversation with Scarlet. I've just been feeling a little lost lately."

He pulled me off of him just enough to look me in the eyes, the curiosity thick in his expression, "How can you be lost when you've never gone anywhere, experienced anything?"

I blinked, knowing he'd find it absurd, but said it anyway. "It's what I haven't experienced that makes me feel lost, empty."

"Jeez, Maggie!" he said as his body shot up from the bed, "What are you talking about?"

"I'm talking about you and Scarlet, mom and dad, Luna and Caleb. Everyone on the block has someone they've found a match with, and it's never going to happen for me because I didn't grow up here like you guys did."

"You're being ridiculous!"

"Whatever, I knew you wouldn't understand. You're being just like Dominic!" I yelled at him, pulling the covers over my head and fighting back the tears that had threatened to surface.

After a while, I felt Devin sit back on the edge of my bed. Being that he hadn't said anything, I removed the covers to find him in the same demeanor he'd been when I woke up.

"I don't want you to feel this way, Maggie, spiraling out of control because of someone else."

"You love her?" I asked him, not really expecting a response but wanting him to be honest with me.

He looked at me, "Maggie, there are day's I don't want to do anything else but be with her and when I'm not here, I can't get home fast enough."

5 THE SMILE

June 2015

Maggie loathed everything about funerals. She'd always felt the gathering to bid farewell to loved ones was done more for everyone else. Deep down, she felt she didn't deserve to be at her grandfather's funeral.

The last thing she remembered telling him was how disappointed she was in him. She recalled how he had sat down from her statement and merely stared at her in shock.

The sad truth was that she wasn't disappointed in him as a grandfather, but as him as a role model. She'd loved him, wanted to be proud of him, and when push came to shove, and the going got tough, he wasn't the man she needed. He threw out ultimatums that pushed her away, and then kept her at arms length.

"How are you hanging in, Niña?" Consuela asked, taking her

in a haphazardly hug.

"I'm peachy, how is Devin? He was the one who actually had a relationship with grandfather," she'd replied, turning her body to face her grandmother more directly.

"He seems to be managing but your brother always had a knack for keeping things to himself," Consuela sighed.

They stood in the center of the funeral home's main room, the open casket not too far away from them, being visited by many people, most of whom Maggie had never seen.

"Who are all these folks?" Maggie asked her, not sure if her grandmother was that involved in their lives.

"Friend's of his. You know how liked he was."

"Yes, but I've only been gone 10 years, I don't know any of these people."

"You know these people, Maggie. They have just changed with age."

Maggie looked around again, this time searching memories of the times she'd spent with Tom. Very slowly she made connections. They weren't strangers, and the memories of him tugged on her heart.

A couple walked into the large room she did recognize, it was Marcy and Wesley, followed by their parents, Norman and Olga.

Maggie smiled at Wesley as their eyes connected. His face lit up, almost as if he hadn't expected to see her there.

He'd let go of Marcy and briskly made his way to where Maggie stood with Consuela. Before any words could be exchanged, he reached out and took Maggie in an embrace.

She didn't shy away from the excitement she felt to see him again. His warmth was a welcomed surprised. She'd worried long ago that when she'd see him, he would hold scorn and regret in his eyes.

In that moment, she searched those light blue eyes again for any resentment, and could find none.

Is it true what they say about time healing old wounds? she thought to herself.

"You are more beautiful than the last time I saw you," he whispered only loud enough for me to hear.

"And, you are still the same old charmer as always."

"Yes well, some things should never change," he teased.

"I'm glad you haven't."

"I'm so glad you came, Maggie. When I heard about Tom, I wondered if you would come. I'd hoped that it would finally bring you home, but I worried about…." His words trailed off. His mind obviously on other memories of what had caused her to leave in the first place, of what keeps her away.

She smiled at him, "Wes, I've missed you so much. You are such a good friend to me. It's been too long."

"Maggie, I wasn't always a good friend and you know it." His grip on her arms tightened, "I was a scoundrel."

"It's all water under the bridge in my book," she squeezed back gently.

He pulled her in for another hug just as Marcy made her way over to them.

"My goodness, haven't you grown up," she sighed at Maggie, looking from her brother to her as though they were doing something inappropriate.

"Marcy, this isn't the time or the place," Wesley sneered at his sister.

"Yes, my condolences to you and your family for the loss of your grandfather," her monotone statement almost sounding rehearsed.

Consuela, who was not too far behind the conversation got closer. "Thank you Marcy. Barbara is over there, I'm sure she would appreciate your presence today," her obvious attempt to remove Marcy from Maggie's presence apparent to everyone standing nearby.

As Marcy walked away, Devin came to stand by his sister.

"Hi Wesley, thank you for coming," his hand reaching out to his old friend.

"Of course, Tom was family."

"Your sister still hasn't grown up, has she," Devin added, the smirk on his face making it clear he was amused by her typical behavior.

"She is who she has always been, I'm afraid," Wesley laughed, watching as Marcy and his parents spoke to Barbara.

His attention turned back to Maggie who was looking at the door, almost waiting for someone.

"You haven't talked to him, I suppose," he asked her, sure she would know to whom he was referring.

Her head snapped back to him, her eyes playing coy. "I'm not sure who you mean."

He huffed softly and his smile returned. He shook his head, "You forget, Maggie, but I know you to the core."

He was right, he did know her to the core. He knew more of her than she would ever want to admit, but in this case she didn't want to admit to still looking over her shoulder to see if Nicholas was near.

"That's fine, you don't have to say anything Maggie," he'd reassured her. "Had you had a chance to talk to Tom before his passing?" he asked, his attempt at changing the subject not doing any good.

"No," she sighed, "I wanted to call him many times but

there never seemed to be a good time. My life has been super crazy busy."

"That doesn't sound exciting, being so busy," he started, "and here we thought being a romance author meant you got to experience a lavish personal life."

Maggie let out a shocked laugh. Of course she would expect Wesley to think something like that about her, but it was a totally different thing for him to admit it freely.

"What, you don't think that's what we all expect? I'm telling you, fact of the matter is, we've all pictured you as this horn-ball sex-o-maniac, being that's all you write about."

"Oh my God, Wesley!" she whispered harshly, "could you be any louder?"

He looked around and noticed that several people were now staring at them. Moreover, Barbara was eyeballing Maggie.

"It's not like we haven't given them something to talk about before" he chuckled under his breath.

Her whole body turned to him at hearing his statement, "Wes, I'm not the same girl I was ten years ago. That is all water under the bridge. I had to grow up and I made something of myself. You, above all others, know this."

He agreed silently to himself, Maggie was not the same girl that left all those years ago. She was someone who had weathered a terrible storm that shaped her into the beautiful vibrant woman who stood before him.

He reached out to her again and pulled her into a hug. "I'm glad you're home, Mags."

The admission brought a genuine smile to her face but as she held Wesley tight she felt herself slip into an old sense of security.

Suddenly, her eyes caught glimpse of a towering figure that entered the funeral home.

It's him, she thought to herself.

Nicholas hadn't wanted to come to old Tom's funeral. He'd held no warm feelings for the man for most of his youth, and yet, there he was, attending the man's wake as if he was meant to be there.

There was a reason for his attendance, and it had everything to do with the long legged beauty now staring at him.

"Wes…" she started, her voice trailing off, the words not forming as her brain stumbled to contain the rapid burst of emotions coursing through her system.

"Before you talk to him, you should know he is married," Wesley warned.

Her eyes met his for a moment but he couldn't tell how she digested the news. Her mouth formed a tender smile while her eyes slowly glistened.

Damn him, Wesley thought, still capable of making her cry.

When she turned to make her way over to where Nicholas stood, he was no longer there.

6 MY SWEET SUMMER
Maggie

July 2002

Abuelita calls it puppy love, Devin, a sick obsession, and Melanie, the love of a lifetime, but I'm not sure who's got it in the bag. I knew by midsummer, however, that I had it bad for Nicholas.

Summer brings lots of things to Carmen Street. Mostly, a renewed companionship amongst the neighbors. At 16, I was too selfish and self-centered to think of anyone other than myself. I hadn't noticed then that Abuelita was slowing down and Devin spacing out. I was only grateful for the freedom that the situation had given me.

Melanie and I spent almost every afternoon at Nicholas' house. Regardless of what our mornings held, we would end up in his driveway playing basketball with the boys and their friends.

The funny part of our routine was the thought they wanted us there. I couldn't tell, especially because Nicholas was just as flirtatious with me and I was with him.

"I bet you can't shoot the ball from this spot," he claimed, walking to the corner of his driveway that butted up to the street.

I mentally measured the distance from where he stood to the last spot I had successfully made a previous shot. When I realized that he had purposefully chosen a distance I had never attempted before, I threw him a deathly glare.

"Why do you do that? Do you like to see me miss?" I sassed him with a smirk.

I'd caught the quick raise of his eyebrow and the lift of the corner of his mouth, the combination of the two signaled he truly was challenging me.

Shaking my head, I walked to where he stood. Bumped my hip to his to shoo him over, the contact of our bodies sending a thousand needy sensations down my legs.

Even if I could make the shot from where we stood, I would never be able to do it with him standing in an intimidating closeness to me. He stared at me, his body facing me and not the hoop, waiting for me to make the shot.

What never surprised me about him was his need to trick me. I raised my arms to make the shot and just as I released the ball, he jumped in front of it stopping it from going any farther.

His laughter infuriated me. It excited me. It halted me to my core, every single time.

Who cared if this wasn't love. It was everything and nothing at the same time. It was random and all consuming.

I charged at him, one arm wrapped around his waist, while the other swatted at the basketball. "That's not fair," I scolded him, but I wasn't angry with him. It was a ploy to be in his arms. He dropped the ball and twisted his body to wrap his arms tight around me. He squeezed until I let out the laughter I'd been holding in.

He laughed with me and pushed me away. The moment he'd let go, I was filled with the want of his touch, his warmth.

I was left panting and out of breath as he stood in front of me laughing. What else could I do but prove him a fool. Turning, I picked up the ball and walked back to edge of the driveway.

Determination has always been my strongest asset. I aimed at the hoop and made the shot. The neighbor boys, Wesley, Marcus and Lucas all called point as the ball swooshed in the net.

What else could I do but look at him and smile.

"How is it that you can do that?" he asked astonished.

My shoulders shrugged as I strutted to the porch where I found my seat.

"I'm just better than you, Nick."

The other boys all laughed and mocked him, a sight that caused me to giggle in delight. I'd won, not just the point but his attention, and theirs for that matter.

I eyeballed him as he walked towards where I sat. His water bottle was on the floor next to me. He picked it up and gulped loudly. The dormant butterflies became unleashed as I focused on the muscles flexing in his arm.

He was doing it on purpose, his eye on me as he drank.

"You know I'm going to win at this rate," the words came out before I could stop myself from taunting him. The close proximity a usual deterrent.

He huffed quietly, his back still to the game. In the background I'd heard the others going about the game, and knew it was nowhere near our turn to shoot.

"Do you think I'm letting you win?" he asked me quietly, his tone low enough for the conversation to be private.

My eyebrows instantly burrowed at him. "Why would you let me win?" the absurdity seething at each word.

Instead of saying anything, Nicholas did what he typically did, he sat on me, and I immediately pulled the girl card. I squealed in disgust from the sweat that now covered my body.

There are two types a sweat a girl accepts, her own, and….well….not this kind.

I shoved at his body but he didn't budge. He laughed and managed to get the rest of the guys to laugh with him.

In the process of fussing at him, I contemplated his purpose.

I was in fact a 'woman in waiting'.

It crossed my mind that he might be pulling such foolish antics to get my attention. Just as I was there, playing basketball, to get his attention.

The thought alone caused me to stop shoving at him, but that only forced him to shift his position to look at me.

"You okay? Am I hurting you?" his concern and his sweetness were the things I adored about him.

"I'm fine but it would be more comfortable if sat on you. I am lighter you know," I teased.

His mouth twitched, the smile trying to come freely. I wondered then about his hesitation. Was it such a big deal for an older boy to have feelings for someone so much younger?

By the end of the month everyone was making plans for the Fall. I'd heard a rumor from Abuelita that Nicholas had been accepted to a collage in North Carolina, Dominic to a college in Georgia and Lucas to a college in North Florida.

"You can't be so surprised, your brother has been talking about it for weeks now," she'd sassed when she brought it up.

"No one said anything about it. This is the first I'd heard about it." The anguish clear in my voice and visible from the immediate pacing.

My eyes shot out the window to see if Nicholas' truck was in his driveway. It was but none of the lights were on in the house.

"I'm going to go talk to Nicholas for a few minutes. I'll be right back," I warned Abuelita on my way out the kitchen door. I heard her holler that I needed to hurry back because dinner was done.

I didn't know what to think, or how to feel for that matter. We'd spent all summer together in one way, shape or form. He even planned on teaching me how to drive.

He was home, I knew that, but what I hadn't realized was that his parent's car was vacant from the garage. Even still, I found myself knocking on the front door.

A chill ran down my spine as I heard him walk up to the door and open it.

"Oh, hey, Maggie. What's up?"

"Are you leaving?" it came out rushed and full of an

emotion I didn't want him to know.

"What do you mean?" Of course he didn't know what I meant, I wasn't being clear, and a part of me didn't even know why it was so important to find out the answer to the question right at that very moment, but there I stood waiting for a response.

"Are you leaving for college somewhere else?"

He stood there, his body even straightened at the question. He knew what I was getting at, and who knows, maybe it was at that moment that he understood my obsession with him.

"I am."

Two words that came down like a jack hammer. I was done for.

My body reacted first, slowly I stepped back, wavering what I was to do.

"Hey," he whispered softly, "come here." He walked out on to his porch, catching me just before I was able to leave.

He pulled my body close to his and wrapped his arms around me.

A tightness overtook my chest and I knew I wanted to cry. I took in the warmth of his hold on me and didn't fight the closeness.

"I don't want you to leave," I whispered into his chest, not worried if he could hear me or not.

"I have to go Maggie."

"You are going to forget about me."

At my words, he gently pulled me away just far enough to look me straight in the eyes. "Maggie, I will never forget you," he started, "I will be back during holidays and breaks. It's not like I'm never coming back."

The absurdity hit me then. He was right. His parents live on Carmen Street, he would be back.

He pulled me back into the hug and held me a little longer.

"Why does it bother you?" he asked finally, letting loose again so I could answer him.

I looked into his green colored eyes and admitted to myself that it wasn't like he didn't know…he probably just wanted to hear it.

"You are my everything, Nick. You have been more these past few years but I know it more certain today, in this moment, than ever before." The moment I'd said it, I found myself shoving my head back on his chest, the embarrassment changing my cheeks to crimson red.

He rubbed my back, holding me a little while longer before letting go completely and walking back to his door.

"I'm not leaving until the end of August, Maggie. We still have time before our sweet summer is gone." The smile on his face meant mischief, and I was fully prepared.

7 HELLO AGAIN

June 2015

Maggie finally caught sight of Nicholas talking to Barbara at the other end of the funeral home. Barbara was smiling, apparently pleased to see him.

"I bet you have a million things running through that beautiful mind of yours, don't you?" Wesley whispered Maggie's ear.

She'd not flinched when she heard his voice, the smooth nature of his presence was often a wonder to her.

"He is exactly the same," she mused, taking note that Nicholas' physical appearance had not changed. He was still the tall handsomely masculine guy he had been 10 years ago. Maybe a little bulkier, but still pleasing to the eye.

"He really isn't though, Maggie," Wesley started. "He's been through a lot these past few years, with his wife and his family. He even...."

Her eye caught Wesley's and he turned back to observe Nicholas.

"He even, what?" she asked, curious as to why he'd hesitated.

"Life didn't stop when you left. You just weren't here."

The statement jolted her.

No, he was right. She wasn't there. She ran away because she was afraid he would never forgive her.

Nicholas turned, making it obvious he was coming to greet them, and while Wesley held a firm smile on his face, Margaret was filled with a dread 10 years in the making.

"Hey man, how have you been?" Wesley greeted his oldest friend with a handshake that was turned into a hug. The two men patting each other on the back.

"Oh, you know, I've been busy with work. It's never a dull moment," Nicholas replied, almost as if making an excuse for his lack of communication.

"I know how it is, Bro."

Their eyes darted to Maggie, both waiting for the words to come out, but she, for the life of her, couldn't say anything.

Nicholas held out his hand to her, "hello again," he offered.

It was the phrase he would say to her every spring when he'd finally come home from college. His way of telling her that he was home.

She smiled in return, the pattern bringing her to a comfort zone she'd only known after hearing those two words come out of his mouth.

"It's nice to see you, Nicholas," placing her hand in his, letting him hold it for a moment.

"I am sorry for your loss. I know how difficult your relationship was with your grandfather."

"Yes, well, it was never peaches and sunshine with Tom. Grandmother says he is at peace now. It's a comfort to know he isn't suffering anymore."

"How have you been?" he asked, casually looking from Maggie to Wesley.

"I've been busy with project after project. While sad a visit this may be, I'm happy for a reason to rest."

"I bet. Every time I realize it, you are putting out a new book," Wesley chimed in.

Maggie nodded, her eyes darting down to the floor. The idea of talking about her work made her uncomfortable.

"You shouldn't worry about what people say, Mags. Everyone is proud of where you are in your life," Nicholas interrupted her thoughts.

Her eyes shot up and met his. "I'm not worried," she snapped in defense.

A smile spread across Nicholas' face, his features now clearly amused. "It's nice to know some things haven't changed."

"I think it's nice that the three of us are in a 5 foot radius of one another and nothings been broken," Wesley jested.

Maggie giggled at Wesley's comment. While he was making light of a difficult situation, it was clear that time had done its job well to make it possible to be standing so close to each other.

"I should go find Abuelita, it looks like the service is going to start," she'd said to the men, reaching out and carefully placing her palm on their forearms.

They both nodded and allowed her to leave without another word, but they both watched her every step as she walked away.

"You okay?" Wesley asked Nicholas.

"I'm probably just as fine as she is, Wes," he'd replied with a sigh.

"She certainly hides it better than you do."

Nicholas turned towards his friend. "You never did get it, did you?"

"What was I suppose to get? She was never mine to begin with," Wesley argued in a hushed tone.

"She wasn't anyone's."

"You're right." Wesley turned his body to face Nicholas'. "But think about this Nick, when I came in, she smiled and all but ran into my arms. When you walked in, her broken heart was written all over her face."

The two men looked back out to the figures now taking a seat in preparation for the service. Maggie glanced back at them and signaled for them to follow suit, the smile on her face heavy with emotions she was trying hard to keep hidden.

Nicholas realized how like the sun she was in all their lives. These past 10 years, they all thirsted the light she'd given so freely as a child. Her warmth and loving touch was gone from their lives, and now that she'd returned, did they realize how much she'd been missed, needed? He did, and it pained him.

The audience listened to several family members give pieces of a eulogy that Thomas had himself requested.

"Your grandmother wants you to say a few words, Margaret," Consuela spoke softly, as her brother was speaking of his childhood.

Maggie could only look at her Abuelita, dumbfounded by such a request.

"It was his dying wish, my dear," she added.

"What beautiful memories can I pull from to comfort his friends?"

"The ones that bring you peace."

"There is no peaceful sail in a torrential hurricane, Abuela. No calm memory to soothe my thoughts about a past I wish to forget."

Consuela did not hide the frown that spread across her face. The bad taste in her mouth caused by words meant for someone else's ears. She looked out to Barbara who was waiting for a signal to hand over the conversation to her granddaughter but only received a negative nod.

Her demeanor changed, which in turn caused her words to seize.

She too frowned at Margaret.

"You know," she began, "a decade ago, our lives were completely different. We did not think of a day such as this. We did not believe that death was knocking at our front door. In being so naïve, our actions did not follow positive progression. Thomas spoke often of his mistakes in this life, you know, in those last few weeks.   All the choices he'd regretted making and moments in which he would have acted differently. But none of those moments resonated more than that which forced our beloved Margaret to leave us."

She was now speaking to Maggie. Her entire speech was directly to her.

"He looked back on when Edward, our son, met Rosa and they had moved away from the neighborhood. He blamed himself for not trying harder to help them get the loan on the house at the end of the street. He said, that had you grown up on that street since you were a baby, everything would have been different," she huffed. "What can I say, in those last few weeks, all he had left was to play the would-of, could-of and should-of game. Thomas was a proud man, he was set in his ways, and as stubborn as they came, but he was a good man."

Her words, 'a good man', struck the wrong chord in Maggie's core. Appropriate or not, Maggie got up and left the room. She walked out of the building and couldn't take a breath until she felt the sun beating down on her face.

Gasping for air as if she'd been underwater, she realized she was having a panic attack. Tears strung down her cheeks and her heart raced frantically.

Revisiting past memories is a messy business. Especially those that didn't turn out all sunshine and roses. Thomas was gone, something no one could change, and in his absence he left a history she couldn't make amends with.

"You okay?" Devin asked from behind her.

Her eyes went to the blue sky now above her.

"No. I'm not okay. I'm the furthest thing from being okay."
She yelled. It was there, the pain, all of it, waiting a decade
to be unleashed.

"Want me to take you home?"

"Home, Devin," she turned to him, "I'm eleven hundred
miles from home."

"I meant, Carmen Street."

8 SPRING BREAK
Maggie

March 2003

Anxious, unnerved and impatient, was how I felt waiting for Nicholas to pull his little black truck into the driveway of his parent's house to start our spring break.

My spring break just so happened to coincide with his, which was great because it was also my birthday weekend.

"Don't you think waiting outside would be more effective?" Melanie suggested.

My head snapped towards her, "a little obvious, don't you think?"

"Oh, Pa-Lease!" her voice dragged. "Everyone in this neighborhood knows what a sick little puppy dog you are after him."

"You make is sound so pathetic, Mel."

Her eyes widened, "it is a little sad, Mags. He is so much

older than you. The only reason he is nice to you and hangs out with you is because you don't give him any other choice."

"That isn't true."

Her hand went up to rest on her hip as she popped it out. "Really?"

I sat back in the blue rocking chair and thought about what she meant.

Could it be, that in truth, he didn't want my company, or didn't want me around?

I'd grown up so used to being around the kids in the neighborhood that I hadn't thought that maybe they would want to exclude me from their time fooling around.

"See, now that you think about it, it makes sense doesn't it?" she reasoned.

All I could do was shake my head at her. I wouldn't agree whole-heartedly but a big part of me felt her reasons were valid, so much so, that when I saw his truck pull in to the driveway of his house, I sat still in my seat.

I'd seen him turn towards my house as he took his bag out of the passenger seat of his truck. For a moment, I wondered if he could see me staring out the window but when he turned and went inside his house I felt it impossible.

That whole first day, I moped around inside the house, only leaving once to get the mail when the carrier drove by.

By dinnertime, I couldn't stand it anymore. I ate and went to sit out on the porch as the sun began to set. The only diversion I could muster was to read a book and act as though I was entertaining myself.

Sure enough, he came outside. Stood at the corner of his porch and stared in my direction.

Was he waiting for me? Had he wanted to see me as much as I ached to see him?

A smile spread across my face as the thoughts swarmed in my head.

We both left our porches and met on the street. I reached out to hug him, and he neither shied nor pulled away. His embrace was affirmation that he was happy to see me too.

"Where were you?" he asked as I looked into his green eyes.

"It doesn't matter anymore. I'm here now."

He turned towards his house and we started walking to his driveway.

"How have you been?"

I couldn't admit how lonely I'd felt, so I lied. "Kinda distracted. School has been busy."

"Any boyfriends?" His question came out quick and I caught his sideways glance as he'd asked but laughed at his question.

"No," I shook my head, "No one of interest in that department." But his question made me wonder.

"How about you? Anyone special at school?"

Please say no, please say no.

His arm wrapped around my shoulder, "Nope, I've been really busy too."

"Well, that is always good to hear," I admitted without thought. My face scrunched, thinking how obvious a statement it had been.

"Oh really," he chuckled.

Out of the corner of my eye, I caught sight of Wesley as he came jogging towards us. Right on time, in my book.

"Hey, Man!" he hollered at Nicholas, giving his friend a guys hug.

"Hi Maggie," he addressed me curtly, reaching out to poke my belly.

"Wesley," I replied, annoyed at being interrupted, and treated like the same ol' little girl by him.

"You want to go out tonight?" Wesley asked Nicholas, obviously excited to have his friend back in town.

"Sure, where you going?"

I listened attentively to their conversation, although Wesley was making it obvious that I wasn't a part of their banter. After a few minutes of planning, Wesley looked at me and grinned, as if satisfied he was taking Nicholas away from me.

"How is your spring break going Maggie?" he eventually asked, sarcastically.

I couldn't help but wonder why Wesley was acting so oddly.

"It's been quiet, but then again no one's been around," I said to Nicholas.

"That's interesting, I've been here the whole time," Wesley blurted out, obviously annoyed by my comment.

He turned to Nicholas who was now staring at me.

"You want to hang out later?" Nick asked me plainly.

The question, while simple, forced my mouth to clamp shut.

I couldn't say no. Wouldn't let Wesley tease me about being a child with a curfew but then again, I was.

I nodded, feeling awestruck by Nick's invitation.

Huffing to distract us, "well, I'm going to go get my keys," Wesley interrupted our moment.

We both watched as he disappeared across the street into

his house.

"You don't have to sneak out if you don't want to. I know why you hesitated," he'd said softly.

I shook my head at him, "It's not a big deal. Abuelita goes to sleep so early."

"Don't mind Wes, he means well. He gets a little full of himself and you are the youngest out of all of us. I'm sure he doesn't understand why we hang out."

"He doesn't really have to, as far as I'm concerned."

"He's my best friend, Maggie. He will figure it out eventually."

A laugh escaped my chest, "And what is there to figure out exactly?" I asked, a part of me wanting to know how he defines our friendship. A little clarification to up the ante.

His foot kicked at a small pebble, his eyes on the ground. I could tell he was contemplating his words.

He shook his head, the playful smile returning to his lips. He was avoiding answering my question. He reached his arms out and poked my belly, just as Wesley had.

Not expecting the touch, I giggle and let him chase me around his front yard. His playful nature distracting me from the primal need to know where we stood.

I fell, being the klutz that I am and landed on his soft plush lawn. He came down next to me on his knees as I pleaded for him to stop tickling me.

"Do you surrender?" his voice demanding and playful at the same time.

"I surrender," I conceded, knowing deep down I would surrender to any of his whims.

"Good," he laughed, helping me up from the ground.

I noticed Wesley returning. "I will see you later." I turned and started walking back home across the street.

"Don't fall asleep," he called out.

Without turning, I raised my arm and tossed him a peace sign.

I'd gone back inside without watching as they left together in Wesley's car.

Abuelita was at the kitchen table when I walked back inside. A disapproving scowl shrouded her wrinkled facial features.

"Ese nino, is not for you, mi-ha."

"His name is Nicholas, Abuela, and it doesn't matter if he is or isn't. He doesn't see me that way, so it's no here or there.

I sat down across from her, waiting for the rest of the argument to in-sue, but she didn't talk of Nicholas.

"Your brother is bringing over his new girlfriend this weekend. He wants us to have a barbeque to introduce her to the neighborhood."

"Wow, that sounds big. What happened to him and Scarlet?" I asked curiously.

"He did not tell me, but I can only assume that it wasn't a good break up. It's only been a few weeks and look, someone new to distract him."

The idea of Devin and Scarlet not being together anymore was a shocker. They'd been together one way or another for as long as I could remember. The idea of them apart was as absurd as if Caleb and Luna were to break up.

"Yikes. I wonder if he is going to invite Dominic?" Abuelita shook her head, not knowing either.

I sighed and wondered about how Scarlet was taking the split. I hadn't seen her around the past few weeks. Could it be because of Devin?

Abuelita and I watched television in the living room that evening until she was too tired to hold her eyes open any longer.

She'd said her goodnight and left me alone watch by myself.

After a good while, I went into the kitchen and quietly took the spare key to the side door off Abuelita's key ring. No one ever used the side door to come in or out of the house, so it wouldn't be a big deal if I unlocked it to sneak out.

Once more I found myself waiting for Nicholas to come home. I sat near the window, absentmindedly flipping the channels, occasionally looking out to see if he was there.

By midnight I was losing hope. My eyes had become tired and I was slowly giving in to the exhaustion.

Fully expecting to go to bed, I turned the TV off and gave one final glance outside.

My heart skipped a beat as I found him standing at the end of his driveway staring in my direction.

There in the darkness of my silent living room, I realized, in that moment, he was waiting for me.

I wanted, more than anything, for him to revel in that feeling. To know what it was like to wait for me, as I had so often waited for him.

What can I say, patience has never been my thing. As quietly and quickly as I could, I unlocked the side door and slipped out into the night.

My mind said to walk, but my feet listened to my heart, and I found myself running into his arms.

He was home and I was in his warm embrace.

"For a second there, I didn't think you were going to come out."

I let out a soft sigh, "for a second there, I didn't think you were coming home."

He pulled me back into a hug and held me a little longer. "All I could think of all night was you sneaking out."

"Oh?" I asked, pulling away from him and walking over to his truck so we could sit.

"I don't want you to get in trouble," he'd admitted, pulling down the hatch.

"I'm fine, she is sound asleep," I said as I took a seat next to him.

"So what did you do tonight?" he asked, changing the subject.

"I watched TV. Where did you guys go?"

His eyes fell to his lap, "We went to Ybor."

"That sounds exciting."

He tossed me a sideways glance, "Not really, it's a glorified meat market."

"A guy like you must not have to try too hard to get a girl to look your way."

He let out a laugh and shook his head, "I'm not looking for any of that right now."

"Me either," I challenged, knowing what he meant.

"So none of the boys have asked you to be their girlfriend?"

"Well, I didn't say that," I laughed, "I am just not looking at the moment."

"See, I knew better. If I was your age, I wouldn't let you look at any other guy," he took my hand in his own.

My heart raced as my eyes fell to the touch I was feeling. His hand covered mine, his fingers caressing my thumb. I could hear the thudding of my beating heart in my ears.

My eyes fluttered up to his just as he leaned towards me, his lips closing in on mine.

I felt myself take in air just as his mouth met mine. The warmth of his breath made me want to shut my brain off, swim in the fantasy my mind had pictured this moment would be. I closed my eyes at that point and let him wrap his arms around me. His lips teases mine a moment until he fully captured my mouth with his.

For the first time in my life I wasn't afraid of anything, of how silly I might be, or how childish I'd always felt.

No, for the first time in my 17 years of existence, I had exactly what I had always wanted....him.

9 RESTING PLACE

June 2015

Much to Devin's surprise, Maggie calmed herself down quickly. He summed it up to the normal nerves that tag along when having to bury a relative.

He kept a keener eye on Maggie as she didn't linger at Tom's grave during the burial. He watched as she walked off into the cemetery, reading the headstones of Tom's dearly departed neighbors. While it was difficult to read any emotions that might be coursing through her system, he could tell that she was finding a reason to be distracted.

Consuela held Barbara's hand tenderly in her own as the old man's casket was inched slowly into the earth. Neither of the two noticed how Maggie was off in her own world.

"How is your sister holding up?" a quiet female voice interrupted Devin's thoughts. He looked down and realized that it was Scarlet, her petite figure dressed in an elegant black dress. She was wearing big designer sunglasses, but he could tell that she had cried a tear or two during the funeral.

"She isn't taking it too well, but you know what the status of their relationship was."

Scarlet nodded, quietly agreeing that she recalled the events that transpired between the two. Everyone did for that matter.

"Poor thing, I can't imagine," Scarlet sighed.

Devin looked out in the distance but this time found Wesley standing just behind his sister. The idea of Wesley coming back into Maggie's life bothered Devin. Call it brotherly love, or just plain common sense. Nothing good ever comes from trouble lingering too close.

Maggie didn't want to leave when Devin suggested it earlier. Mostly because she refused to give anyone something else to talk about. Her mere presence was enough to keep their tongues wagging for a while.

The cemetery was a whole other ball of wax, however. She couldn't quite explain what was worse, the fact that she hadn't been able to suck up her pride or make time to amend things better between Tom and herself or the mere realization that everyone in her current surrounding knew she hadn't made amends with him.

"When I die, I want to be cremated," Wesley's soft voice startled her. Turning, she found him standing only a few feet from her.

Her eyes wide, "I didn't hear you."

"I can see that. I'm sorry, I don't mean to intrude. I just saw you wandering off and it reminded me of...." He trailed off, breaking eye contact with her.

"Some things never change do they?" she smiled.

"Which things? You wandering off, or me following you to make sure you are okay?"

The smile inched slowly at the memories he was invoking. "I suppose both".

"I don't regret any of it, you know that don't you?" he admitted baldly.

"We couldn't change any of it if we wanted to. It's made us who we are, puts us where we are."

He lifted his hand out towards her to take. "I've missed you Mags, more than I could ever say."

"Let's not say and act as though we had," she teased, making it clear she couldn't go there with him.

He returned her smile and sighed as she placed her hand in his, allowing their fingers to intertwine.

71

Off in the crowd, Nicholas watched intently as his best friend comforted the bane of his existence. His stomach churned as Wesley touched her, held her, and became good friends as before.

He'd known he'd see her, but desperately begged it wouldn't affect him the way it currently was. Looking into her eyes earlier was like having a knife stab his heart a thousand times over.

But why wouldn't it, she was, after all, the love of his life. The one person he was, still to this day, trying to forget but poorly succeeding.

And there she was, off in the distance, once more in the arms of the man he considered a brother. History was seemingly repeating itself.

"Tell me you are not pining away for that little witch," Wesley's sister, Marcy, scolded.

Nicholas shook his head, not wanting to play into her disgust. He'd known since they were young that Marcy hadn't approved of the friendship between them.

"I'm married Marcy. I have been for quite some time now."

She huffed under her breath, as she adjusted her sunglasses. "I've heard rumors about your marriage, Nick, and I'm sure Margaret has too. Just make sure she doesn't bring my brother down again like she did the last time."

Nicholas slightly turned his body to face Marcy, "Wesley is my friend, and while we may have had our differences as young boys, we have come a long way in mending that friendship. She wasn't completely to blame in what happened, and you damn well know that." He seethed at her in a low tone only she could hear.

When Marcy lifted her chin to him, he decided it was time to go on a walk of his own, away from the crowd all together.

Maggie noticed Nicholas heading towards his truck near the back of the car line.

"I wonder what has him off in a huff," she sighed.

Wesley realized, by the manner his friend was walking, that his friend was upset.

"I'll be right back."

She let go of Wesley's hand and watched him make his way to Nicholas before he had a chance to get in his truck.

Wondering if it was as hard on him as it was on her, Maggie turned back to the cemetery where the crowd was now breaking up. The service was over.

The time for goodbye had long past, and there she stood wishing nothing more than to hug the old man and say she was sorry for every terrible thing she had ever said to him.

Consuela made eye contact and gave a gentle nod. It was

Scarlet that walked towards her though.

"Maggie, you look beautiful as always," she greeted, reaching out to hug her old friend.

"You too, Scarlet. I'm so happy I had a chance to say hi."

Scarlet tilted her head in confusion, "you don't mean to say you are leaving, do you?"

"With everything, I think it would be best if I just went home."

"No, you can't leave yet. Everyone is going to be home this week. I heard Consuela is having a dinner like old times."

Maggie dropped her head in defeat and shook at the mere idea of getting around to seeing everyone.

"Maggie, I can't imagine what you are going through but we are family, like it or not and the past is long gone. We love you and want you to be well. Just let us in again."

Maggie looked at her friend and didn't know what to say. She was preaching to the choir quite frankly. Maggie just had to give in to things she couldn't change.

"Fine. You win. I will stay a little longer but I have to leave eventually."

"Well, then, let's hope eventually isn't any time soon." She closed the distance and hugged Maggie.

"Where is Melanie? I haven't had a chance to talk to her,"

Scarlet asked, looking around the crowd getting ready to leave.

"I'm not sure, exactly," Maggie admitted sheepishly, knowing she should have been with Melanie throughout the service.

She didn't find Melanie until she arrived back at Abuelita's house. Consuela and Devin made it a point to keep silence the entire drive back home. It suited Maggie just fine. There were too many thoughts dancing around in her mind.

"Where were you?" she asked Melanie when she found her sitting at the kitchen table flipping through a magazine.

Melanie's eyes slowly lifted to meet Maggie's and she quickly realized that Melanie was annoyed.

"You do realize that Wesley looks like he is following you around like a teenage boy, don't you?" Melanie lashed out.

"Oh My God, Melanie, back to this again? It's been 10 flipping years. Let it go already." Maggie raised her voice, throwing her arms up in the air, as she left the kitchen and stormed into the living room.

Melanie bolted out of the chair she was sitting in and followed her cousin, ready to argue her point.

"Yeah, 10 years, but damn it to hell if you haven't learned from your mistakes."

"My mistakes!" she shot back, turning around to meet her cousin's glare. "Look who's talking, Mel."

"I don't want to fight with you, Mags," she sassed, her hand planted firmly on her hip.

"Then leave it be."

Melanie shook her head that she wouldn't. Defiant as she'd always been.

"Fine, then what do you want me to do? What do you want me to say?" Maggie pleaded, needing it to be said clearly to her.

"I'm still in love with Wesley, Maggie. I have been since I was a child. Just like you were with Nicholas."

"I didn't steal Wesley away from you Mel. We made a mistake and we both paid for that mistake."

"Paid for it? Are you kidding me, humiliation isn't payment."

At that moment, Maggie realized something crucial, "you don't even know do you?"

Melanie's face when blank, "know what?"

Maggie sat down on the sofa and clasped her hands on her lap. "Melanie, Wesley and I got pregnant."

The shock on her face made it clear that not everything was as it seemed. Not everyone knew the true disgrace of the whole situation.

Melanie found herself sitting next to Maggie. The shock not having worn off yet. "Oh my," she said softly.

"Yeah, Oh my, indeed. But we can't talk about this right now. Abuelita needs us to help her finish getting ready for this dinner she is planning. There is no reason to get into all that."

Maggie got up and looked out the living room window and found a familiar figure standing at the end of his driveway, talking to old friends. She knew from experience that Nicholas could in fact see her staring out at him but it didn't make her feel any better. It didn't erase the memory of how badly she'd hurt him. Of all the beauty he had created in her life, all of which she'd ruined in the blink of an eye.

"They both still love you, Mags," Melanie said from behind her.

"Which doesn't make it any easier, Mel."

10 MY LITTLE LOVE
Maggie

May 2004

Far be it from me to admit to any form of trouble to anyone other than those in my inner most trusted circle of friends and family, but I had to a new friend who turned out to be a refreshing new addition to my life. Someone I'd come to trust in a way I didn't think I was capable of trusting, his name was Adam.

He'd registered at school a few months ago. Making everyone wonder why anyone would go to so much trouble as to see out the last few months of their senior year, especially when he could have just received his diploma at the end of his last semester in New Haven, CT.

He'd sat down in our 3rd period class on his first day and basically watched me the entire 45 minutes. From the very start, I knew there was something about him, I just couldn't put my finger on it.

The handsome teenager effect suited him well. His dark hair and piercing blue eyes made him a magnet for all the available girls, even the unavailable girls were pausing to question their attraction to him.

We became quick friends, Adam and I, and his friendship was what got me through Nicholas' absence. He'd become a welcomed distraction. Someone I could look at and talk to that didn't remind me of what my heart was aching for.

Melanie and Wesley both hated the new friendship. They'd made it clear by keeping me out of the loop regarding a few upcoming neighborhood social affairs.

Had it not been for Devin and Abuelita, I wouldn't have known that everyone was getting together to celebrate Melanie and my upcoming graduation.

"What is it with her lately?" Devin had asked me, nonchalantly flipping the channels of the living room television.

"She is sour with me because of Adam." I stated plainly, making it clear how ridiculous it sounded.

"She has been spending an awful lot of time with Wesley lately, hasn't she? Maybe his bad manners are rubbing off onto her."

"*A lot more than bad manners*." I thought to myself. I would never 'out' Melanie, but she'd put herself out there and found a morsel of happiness.

"Is Nicholas coming down for your graduation?" Devin asked, pausing his flipping of channels to gauge my reaction to the question.

I merely met his gaze and shrugged my shoulders. Fact was, I didn't know if he was coming or not. He hadn't called, sent any letters, and quite frankly I was annoyed.

"Well, at least you have Adam," he sighed.

"As if Adam is a consolation prize." I stood, upset, because he'd gone ahead and thrown Nick and Adam in the same subject and made a mess of my thoughts.

"That's not what I meant, Mags," he shouted and stalked out of the living room and all the way out of the house.

Florida's May humidity surrounded my exposed skin. I looked up to the sky and spread out my arms soaking in the sunlight. The momentary silence soothing all the jumbled emotions.

That was to say, very momentary. A honk from down the street took me out of the peaceful state and sent me down a whole other staircase of hell.

Grandma Barbs and Papa Tom where sitting in their grey Lincoln Town car in the front driveway of their house staring at me.

"Want to come to the store with us?" he called out from his car window.

I smiled at him but shook my head that I didn't. "Sorry Papa, I'm busy this afternoon," I lied to him.

"Alright, suit yourself," he said as he raised the glass and backed out of the driveway.

I watched as they left and Wesley walked out of his house. He caught sight of me and waved with a smile.

The smile he held was more than just mischievous, it was downright suspicious.

"What are you up to?" I called out, deciding I would go talk to him for a moment.

"Why do I always have to be up to something, with you?"

"You forget how well I know you Wesley," I giggled at his contrite demeanor. He wasn't upset, he was baiting me to ask what he was doing.

"Well, out with it then," I demanded, eyebrow raising just a tad to ensure he was checkmated.

"I can't win with you can I?"

I smiled, but only because I'd never thought of it as a game. "No, you can't but I'm willing to let you try," I teased.

"You minx!" he laughed and initiated a chase. I ran but realized he wasn't going to give up so I let him catch me. His arms wrapped around my waist and we fell to the ground. He tried to tickle me but I wiggled out of his hold and got up on my knees.

"We are too old for this, Wes," I said, the laughter still in my voice.

"We're never too old to have fun with friends, Mags."

His statement tugged on my heart. "Why is Melanie being so hard on me, Wes?"

"I didn't realize she was," he admitted as he helped me up to my feet again.

"I think she is mad that I'm friends with Adam but I can't fathom the why behind it."

"Well, she has voiced her opinion about that a few times. She said you wouldn't like it if Nicholas had a cozy friend that was a female."

My eyes shot to the grass. "Like it would matter if I knew anyway," I mumbled under my breath.

Wesley reached out and gently raised my chin with his forefinger to look at him, "If he did, it would matter."

I shook my head at him, my eyes pooling with tears I dared not shed in his presence. I wanted him to think I was strong enough to stomach such things. I turned and started to walk away.

He was right behind me the first few steps and stopped me by the third. "It matters, Mags," he repeated, this time turning me around and taking me into his strong arms. His hold on me was almost protecting me from the emotions just under the surface.

"I'm no good missing him, Wes," I whimpered into his chest.

"It will be over soon, sweetie. He will be home before you know it," he said, caressing my back as he held me. We stood like that for what felt a lifetime, until I stopped crying and was able to breathe normally again.

"Better?"

I pulled away and looked at him. The features of his face made him seem sincere, soft and caring, even.

"Good enough," I replied, pulling away just far enough to feel my own strength taking over.

"Tell me something Maggie."

"Shoot."

"Why him?" he'd said it in a manner which contradicted the friendly banter we'd always shared. Was he challenging my feelings for Nicholas?

The question forced a wedge between us.

"As opposed to whom, exactly? You?" I met the challenge, though gently placed, head on.

"Why not?"

The raised eyebrow indicated he was testing me.

"He was there first."

"Was he now?"

"He was. I was important to him when loose girls and beer were important to you. He came home to see me, be with me, and give his attention to me, I didn't know where you were off to."

"You forget, my little love, that he'd been with me, chasing those loose girls and drinking those tasty beers before he'd come home every single night to you."

My spine straightened, and my demeanor changed. He was right, at the core I knew he was, but still, he was baiting me to think twice.

"I don't understand you, Wesley. One minute you are so good to me, and the next you are this....this guy that searches for the deepest cut to sting."

"You think Nicholas doesn't already know about Adam? Think again Mags. He knows, and he isn't happy about it. So while you sit there and think him to be the best of the best because he paid attention to you, remember everyone else that pays attention to you and is straight forward with you, because at the end of the day, the truth you hold on to is the truth that makes you who you are..."

His words became errant, he grasped my upper arms and held me, forcing me to hear his words. An inexplicable pain clear in his cracking voice. "I have been here Mags, for the past 3 years I haven't left. I've been here, right effing here. I never left. I see your face every God forsaken day, and I give you the attention you crave, every single time."

I twisted out of his grasp, "What are you talking about?"

"You don't see it do you?"

"Melanie, Wesley. Melanie loves you," I said, my arms wrapping around my stomach.

"What difference does that make when you are standing right in front of me," he boldly admitted.

"Oh, my God, Wes. What's wrong with you?" I shouted at him. My heart racing from the absurdity that was spewing out of his mouth. My mind spun from the whole scenario that, for a moment, I wondered if this was just a nightmare.

"I can't…" I started, backing away from him, making sure he couldn't reach out to grab a hold of me again. "Nicholas is your best friend, like your brother. This is insane."

Turning, I found my feet racing, matching the pulsating in my heart. I didn't run home, I ran to the end of the street, turned and headed towards the nearby park. Tears were streaming down my face at a terrible rate.

I missed Nicholas, and now I would endure the loss of Wesley because of this nonsense. Melanie would surely come to despise me, everything was in shambles.

I sat on a bench just inside the park, very near the road and cried into the palms of my hands.

I hadn't expected anyone to see me, mostly because I hadn't been thinking at all. Devin must have been driving by when I came into view. He pulled over and called out to me as he got out of his car.

"What's wrong?" he asked, walking towards me.

I looked up and realized I had scared him. The tears on my face probably didn't help matters.

"Nothing, just go home," I told him, my voice cracking from the sob still stuck in my chest.

"Go home? Really, and leave you like this? Tell me what's wrong," he demanded.

"It's ruined Devin. Everything is messed up."

His armed wrapped around me and he pulled me close to him. His chest taking in a deep breath.

"What's ruined Maggie?" he asked softly.

I had to get it off my chest, otherwise it would eat away at me until I had no strength to hold it in.

"Wesley all but told me he is in love with me."

I felt how Devin shook his head in disregard, his muscles sharply tightening, and his heart thudding harder in his chest.

"Well that isn't surprising, I suppose. He always had it in him to go ruining a good thing."

"He is one of my best friends, Devin. I'm going to lose both of them."

"So be it, you lose both of them. It isn't the end of the world. Life moves on, love happens again."

"Is that how you feel about Scarlet?" I asked him spitefully.

"No, I don't, and that is completely different."

"Is it? You were best friends, lovers, and then one day, it's over. You can't tell me it doesn't hurt to lose someone that's more than just a love. She was a part of your world, the sun that made everything bright. Don't you see, Wesley and Nicholas are the sun and the moon is my life. I can't live without either."

"You have no idea what you can and cannot live without, Margaret. You are stronger than you give yourself credit for and you're scared because just maybe, Wesley is right."

11 MAGPIE

June 2015

Melanie having the courage to admit her feelings for Wesley struck home. Maggie had written about courage and strength and love for so many years but it seemed to pale in comparison to how it is in real life.

Melanie had stood there, conviction in her armor, and told her well kept secret to the one person she thought could ensure she'd have her happily ever after. The truth was a totally different matter. Melanie admitted her feelings to Maggie so that she would back down from any internal claims to him, or his heart. It was a selfish act she hoped didn't backfire in her face.

Melanie prayed that Maggie's love for Nicholas was still haunting her, even though he was married now, that wouldn't be an obstacle for very long.

"So, what are your plans for this dinner, Abuelita?" Maggie asked Consuela as Melanie came back into the kitchen.

"My plans were to bring this family back together but if you two can't be on good terms then I think it is futile to even suggest such an eventful evening." The old woman still had her wits about her.

"Yes, well, I think Melanie and I will be just fine. The past is many things but not one to change in its nature," she said it with hopes that Melanie would drop the subject.

"Bueno let's make a list then. A trip to the store will be in order."

"How many people are you expecting Abuelita?" Melanie asked, amused by her grandmother's gleeful demeanor.

Consuela mentally counted, lifting her hands to count, then shook her head several times to start again, "Maybe 70 or so, I am still waiting to see if the new people at the end of the street acknowledge my existence."

Shocked, "You invited everyone?" Maggie all but shouted.

Satisfied she had gotten her grand-daughter's full attention, "Si, everyone. Let them all come and celebrate my baby being home," she reached out and took Maggie's face in the palms of her hands.

"You make me so happy, Margarita Mia!"

"I love you too, Abuelita."

"So this list?" Melanie interrupted, pen and paper in hand.

That night, Maggie couldn't fall asleep. She'd tossed and turned until the sheets were entirely on the floor. The fan was spinning tirelessly but her body was flushed.

The memories of Nicholas and Wesley swam in a sea of torrential waves that she couldn't lay to rest. She threw on a satin robe and quietly made her way through the silent house. The only noise was Abuelita's snore coming from behind her closed bedroom door.

She went to the kitchen and poured herself a glass of water. While it was refreshing to drink, it did little to settle her nerves. She walked into the living room, feeling the pull of the window, and took a look towards the street.

Not expecting to see anything, she began to look away when something caught her eye. A flickering light and a man's figure stood on Nicholas' porch.

Could it be him? She asked herself.

Waiting just a moment longer meant she would contemplate another action all together, one she'd taken many times over the years. She was definitely one to throw caution to the wind and jump head first into a moment.

She found herself biting on her bottom lip and drumming up the same excuses that never held up. The ultimate decision was made in which she went in search for the side door key that Abuelita now hid above the doorframe.

It was easy to open and close a door, it was altogether something more challenging to walk across a dark street in your night clothes to meet an old flame.

He came off the porch the moment he realized she was walking down her driveway. He paused only one instant to take in how his heart rate changed when he realized she was coming out to see him. Not wanting to get excited, especially since he was still so very confused, he took his time to make his way to greet her. When she reached the edge of her grandmother's driveway, he noticed she didn't have any shoes on and was dressed in her nightgown.

His stomach turned, and he jogged to where she was standing. Her beautiful brown hair flowing over her shoulders, caressing parts of her he dreadfully couldn't forget.

He hadn't forgotten those parts of her. Like her currently bare legs that radiated beauty in the moonlight. How they once wrapped around his waist with an urgency in which most men could only dream of.

"Hi," she whispered when he stopped only feet in front of her.

"Hi back at you," he smiled casually.

She shook her head and looked up to the moon. "Beautiful night."

His eyes never left her though, he watched as she deflected from her current frame of mind, her state of being.

When she looked back into his eyes, she could tell he had a lot on his mind.

"I'm sorry, Nicholas."

He found his head nodding once, and then his mouth piercing, followed by an involuntary sigh. All of which felt more like someone else than the man he'd become.

"Sorry about what exactly," he heard himself say.

Her expression hardened, her emotions going from sad to alert. Defensive. He'd gone and sent her into defensive mode, which if he recalled back, that wasn't the way to get her to open up.

"You know, I was laying in bed, tossing and turning all night. Maybe it was the guilt I'd been feeling all this time because of what happened all those years ago, but maybe I was wrong."

"No, I think you were right. It was guilt. But hell, call it what you want. Who knows, maybe you just wanted to see if I was still pining over you Magpie," the sharpness of his tone was not surprising.

She stilled at the sound of his term of endearment for her. He was angry, seething with hurt, and still he called her Magpie.

10 years of longing hit her like a ton of bricks. She reached out and kissed him.

While surprised as he may have been, he reacted as only any other man in Maggie's life ever did in moments like that. He gave back what she was giving willingly.

His arms wrapped around her figure and he kissed her with a passion he'd never had with any other woman, not even with his wife. The want was in every flick of his tongue, every touch of her soft bare skin. His hands reached into her hair and he could feel the tightness in his groin reach a crucial peak.

She let out a low moan of desire, which sent him reeling. She was his so long ago, he wanted her to be his once again, even though he was still angry with her.

He pulled away gently, his tongue caressing the outer line of her lips. He teased her, but it only created more longing, something which drove her to slide her hand down his chest and to the heat growing within his jeans.

Her eyes opened to see his reaction as she rubbed the material that housed the growing anguish.

The fire had been set ablaze, not a single thing would put it out but one simple act. He would take her and let the cards fall where they may. Capturing her mouth again, he did nothing to stop her.

She rubbed his length, knowing full well what it was doing

to him. Knowing deep down that there was only one way this would end.

Her own need was calling, she could feel the wetness in excess, her body needing him to take charge as he'd done so many times before.

She closed her eyes as his mouth moved down her neck and to the soft material covering her breast. He pulled the delicate fabric away, taking a pink nipple into his mouth, suckling and tasting her warm skin.

When he pulled away to look at her, her eyes were half open, her mouth wanting, and her hands lay softly on his chest.

"Tell me this is what you want," he whispered, his heart aching to hear her say those three words once more.

She didn't have to think, her body was doing all the answering for her. "I want you," she whispered.

He took her hand and led the way across the street to his parents' house.

"Wait, your parents" she paused just before they went into the house.

"They have trouble hearing on good days. Aside from the fact that their room is on the other side of the house, I have a lock on my door, remember?"

The soft smile returned to her face, he was right. This

wasn't the first time they were sneaking in.

Walking in to his bedroom brought on a wave of nostalgia. She'd given her heart to him in this room, her virginity.

"You're a little over dressed don't you think?" she teased him and watched intently as he removed his t-shirt, discarding it on the floor near the bed.

She climbed onto the other side of the bed and staying on her knees, as she nudged closer, watching as he unbuckled his pants letting them fall to the floor as they exposed the very core of his desire. His need for her was much greater than she had imagined, time playing tricks on her memory.

"Now it's you that's over dressed, my sweetness."

She giggled at his playful demeanor, but realized as he kneeled onto the bed as she had, that he would readily correct the clothing issue on his own.

His masculine hands tugged on the satin tie that kept her robe so perfectly on her. She held her breathe for a moment as he bent to kiss her breast as he removed the robe from her shoulders. The soft material felt divine as it landed on the backs of her legs and feet.

All that was left was her thin pink nightgown and she would be as bare of clothing as he was.

His hands lowered to the hem of her nightgown and he slowly pulled it up, revealing her naked skin. He removed it, taking her mouth once their hands were both high in the air. As he tossed the material across the room, his arms wrapped around her and he pulled her tight up against his body. His throbbing manhood gently pressed against the very place he would soon venture towards claiming.

His hands caressed the soft skin of her back, and their kiss became greedy.

"I can't take this much longer," she groaned as his mouth went to her neck again.

She fell to the bed and stared up at him. Her hair sprawled all about, she looked like a goddess and he was powerless in her mist. Or was she a witch who enchanted him into falling in love with her all over again.

"I need you," she pleaded softly, her words bringing him down to lay on top of her. Her legs wrapped around his waist as he propped himself up on his elbows to look into her eyes.

"You are so beautiful, Maggie," he whispered as he thrust himself deep inside her. A gasp escaped her lips but he didn't stop, he kissed her again and everything faded away. All he could feel was her wetness, the heat from her skin, the passion in the way her mouth met every kiss. Her hands grasped his back, holding on to him, while her heels dug into his buttocks forcing him to dive deeper and deeper.

He reached the edge of that abyss she'd taken him to many times but this time he opened his eyes and watched as she soared into rapture, her climax bringing her limbs to quiver beneath his body. His body yielded to her will and he followed her lead, crying out her name into the night and giving in to his own blissful release.

He fell next to her, pulled her into his body and he tenderly wrapped his arm around her. Sleep took them.

12 GRADUATION
Maggie

June 2004

Devin's words resonated for several weeks before they finally sunk in and I understood the full meaning of what he was saying.

Wesley was acting out a selfish need to admit to such feelings for me. The question I still held a firm grasp on was if he would ever act on those emotions he said were running rampant through his system.

Either way, Nicholas was his best friend, the love of my life, and I wouldn't do anything to compromise that relationship. It's why I stopped spending so much time with Adam. Wesley was right, and quite frankly, so was Melanie. I wouldn't like it one bit if I heard that Nicholas was spending quality time with another female. No matter how platonic it may be, the little time we have together is not enough to feel satisfied by such a knowledge.

I sent him a letter, explaining my friendship, and while innocent it may have been, it seized to prosper.

With school being at an end, and that walk across the graduation stage looming about, I doubt it made any difference anyhow. It is common knowledge that high school friends are a passing fancy, they linger ever so long, but eventually fade into a memory of a time that changed you, made you who you are.

The neighborhood, on the other hand, was a completely different story. Abuelita had been planning this graduation party that was to take place right after the event itself, where of course everyone was said to be participating. Even Luna and Caleb, now married, were flying in from Georgia to celebrate with us.

All Mel could think about was how her dress was going to fit and what songs she was going to make sure our D.J. cousin, Alyssa, played. Making sure to add a few slow songs so that she could entice Wesley to dance with her.

I, on the other hand, can't get this sinking feeling that something horrible was going to happen. I had asked Nicholas' brother Austin, when I saw him earlier this week, if he knew if Nick would be home, seeing as how the college semester was over, but Austin had no clue. Either that or he was sworn to secrecy.

It was nerve racking to be in limbo, not knowing what the next few days would hold. Forget about the future, the next few days would be the start of my future.

The morning of graduation, Abuelita walked into my bedroom and sat at the corner of my bed as I stretched and blinked my eyes opened.

"Good morning," I smiled at her. Her features, while wrinkled, were refined and delicate. I hope to hold an ounce of her beauty when I'm her age.

"Buenos Dias, good morning my sweet," she replied and reached out to touch my hand. "Did you sleep well?"

"Good enough, I suppose."

She nodded and glanced at my bedroom door.

"Is everything okay?" I asked her cautiously, an inner alarm stirring me awake further.

"You have a visitor, my dear."

Instantly I was sitting up and tossing the covers off of myself. It had to be him, it had to be.

Like a little girl on Christmas morning, I ran out of my bedroom, down the hall, and into the living room, only pausing a moment to affirm what my heart was telling me.

Nicholas was home, smiling at me with his arms held out to me.

I ran and jumped into his arms, my legs wrapping around his waist as he twirled me around. Every ounce of my soul was blissfully complete. Right then and there, there was no other happiness that compared.

"Oh, I have missed you," he whispered in my ear, kissing my neck, my cheek, and then my lips.

There were misty little tears in my eyes, and when he pulled away to see me he gently wiped them away.

"I'm here now."

"And I'm the happiest girl in the world for it," I said, hugging him again. His arms holding me just a tad tighter than he'd ever held me.

Finally, I pulled away and found my feet once more on the ground. "When did you get in?" I asked.

He took my hand and sat next to me on the sofa. "I got in just about an hour ago. I didn't want to wake you too early today but I couldn't wait any more. I hope you don't mind?"

"I could never mind waking to see your face, Nick." I said it and felt the meaning transforming into something I hadn't even thought of until the change in his expression.

"I mean..." I tried to explain but he raised a forefinger to grace across my lips.

"Don't. Let it stay there, that thought of what you didn't mean. Because I haven't been able to think of anything else since the last time I laid eyes on you."

I could feel the flush of heat reach my cheeks, and a tingle in my stomach dancing a very rhythmic dance.

Abuelita cleared her throat and both of our faces shot in her direction.

"Tell me Nicholas," she began, "Now that are done with your schooling, what are your plans?"

His face turned to me, "I plan on asking Margaret to marry me."

Shock.

My mouth fell open, but words were trapped in the pit of somewhere farther below my stomach.

Yes, I mentally yelled at him, but nothing came out. Not even a croak.

Let's just assume that his reaction was based on my lack of words...

"That is, when she is ready, of course," he directed to Abuelita.

My eyes shot to her, praying she would agree, because the moment the words returned I fully planned on screaming yes a thousand times over.

"That will be for her to decide, Nicholas. Currently, however, Margaret has a big day ahead of her that has nothing to do with vows but a future of promise.

Nicholas nodded casually to her, and then looked back to

me. Absurd as I may have looked, he kissed me on the forehead and found his way out of the house.

She shook her head at me, "what is wrong with you?"

I blinked, releasing the breathe I hadn't even realized I was holding and jumped to my feet.

"Oh my God," I shouted, "he asked me to Marry him," I squealed.

My feet reacted before I could think of what I was doing. I ran out of the house and into the front yard. He turned, at the end of the drive way, and for the second time took me into his arms.

"Yes, Yes, I will marry you." I shouted gleefully, and began placing kisses all over his face.

"For a moment there, I didn't know what to think Magpie. You had me worried."

I pulled away and looked up into his beautiful green eyes, "You have been my everything since I was 10 years old. Why would you ever think I would say no?"

That was when it hit me…he'd talked to Wesley.

"Maggie, it's just…" he trailed off.

I inched away, only far enough to grasp a few of my bearings so I could consider his standpoint.

"I don't want you to feel like I'm taking everything away

from you."

"What would make you think that?" I asked, praying the answer had nothing to do with his best friend.

"I have been away for such a long time. You've lived a whole other life apart from when I'm with you. I don't know where I fit in to your life."

"I could say the same thing, Nick," I gently argued back.

"It's different, you were here with everyone else."

"Everyone as in Wesley?"

"Everyone as in Carmen Street."

"I didn't choose that, Nicholas," I shot back.

"I know you have feelings for Wesley," he boldly stated.

There it was.

I took two steps back, the words more like a slap in the face than a truth he'd been holding on to.

"I don't love him."

He nodded his head once, accepting my words but I could tell it still wasn't enough.

"Is that why you asked me to marry you? To test me, my love for you?" the question seemed to come out without merit.

When he said nothing, my worst fear was realized.

"Don't come today....better yet, just don't come to any of it," I said, the tone in my voice sounding alien.

"Maggie..." he tried to talk but I held my hand up to him, stopping him.

"Don't." I backed away, turned and went back into the house. I went straight back to bed, pulled the covers up to my cheeks and let the tears that had begun to well up, the moment I was no longer facing him, fall.

Everything hurt, every limb in my body quivered as I sobbed the morning away. Somewhere along the line I fell asleep, a dark abyss comforting my weak heart.

It was mid-afternoon before Abuelita came back into my room.

"Mi-ha, you are going to miss it if you don't get dressed now. Melanie is in the living room waiting for you to leave together."

There was an idea, miss it all, stay under the covers and block out the life that meant everything to me.

She must have realized that I was contemplating the idea. "You can't start the rest of your life by giving up when the going gets tough."

When I met her gaze, her face softened. "I love you, Abuelita."

"Get dressed. You don't want to disappoint Melanie. She so excited, she is pacing. I swear she will be tired before she even gets there."

The idea caused me to giggle, it would be something Melanie would do.

"Are you ready?" Melanie asked me as we reached the steps to cross the stage.

"As ready as I will ever be." I replied thankful to know she was going first.

The moment I walked across that stage, with thousands of friends and family members gathered in the enormous auditorium, I felt invigorated, like the world was at my feet.

Nicholas didn't listen to my wishes, I met his gaze a time or two when searching the crowd for other familiar faces. His jaw line was stern, and unchanging. Amazingly enough, Wesley sat next to him, beaming with pride.

While it unnerved me to see the two of them so close together, knowing the truth under the surface of his heart, I couldn't imagine him missing this day.

That night, amongst familiar faces and happy laughs, Wesley made no attempt to interact with me. For once I was thankful for the disinterest.

Nicholas sat next to Devin the entire night. Occasionally, he would have a conversation with an old friend but he mostly sat broodingly staring at me as I danced and mingled with everyone other than him.

"What is wrong with Nicholas tonight?" Scarlet asked me when she caught me glancing at him as he stared at me.

I turned towards her, giggling at what she might be suggesting, "I haven't the faintest clue," I lied.

Her eyebrow rose, "Really? because he has that look about him like he is ready to strangle you."

I turned at gave him a look over, thinking if her words fit his current expression, then I looked back to her, "You know, you're right!" I laughed out loud, feeling the night air taking over my light demeanor.

"I need a walk. I'll be back in a little while." I told her, leaving before she could say another word.

My feet knew exactly where to take me. The bench in the park on the adjacent street had become a tiny refuge since Devin found me there weeks ago.

I sat and realized I had been followed. The moonless night giving the streetlights liberty to dance shadows of their own.

It was Nicholas. His tall lean figure undeniable no matter the light. When he came into full view, he paused, waiting for me to say something.

"Tell me you love me no matter what," I boldly asked him.

Wordless movements brought him to sit next to me. "I will always love you no matter what."

And with that, I forgave him.

13 A NEW DAY

June 2015

Maggie woke tangled in Nicholas' arms. The sound of his heavy breathing signaled that he was still asleep. She took a moment to revel in her surroundings. Being in Nicholas' arms felt right, it always had. No other man she'd ever met left her feeling whole, complete.

She'd managed to make a full circle. It was very like them to argue and end up in bed; like being privy to a secret dance, in which, only they knew the melody and special steps.

He stirred, his eyes fluttered open as he felt her warm soft skin laying atop his chest. Without looking into her eyes, he recalled the events that lead to their current embrace.

By which his eyes firmly closed, quickly signaling regret to register. What had he done? He'd made love to her. As if he hadn't been confused enough as it was, now he would have to contend with recalling how it felt to touch the siren in present day. The memories were haunting but this would be far more difficult to push out of his mind.

The moment he tensed up, Maggie felt the urgency to leave. The only thing holding her back was his grasp on her midsection. It was slowly becoming too difficult for her to keep her breathing even.

"I think I'm going to need to borrow something to wear," she deflected.

Remembering that he dragged her across the street, barefoot and in her nightgown, he agreed making that walk back to her grandmother's house would need an extra few pieces of clothing, seeing as the sun was now rather high in the sky.

"You always did end up taking my clothes, didn't you?" he found himself teasing her. The lighthearted tone of his voice contradicted the torrential storm of emotions waging war in his heart.

She used his chest to push herself to sit up, the pressure forcing him to look at her.

'God, how can she be more beautiful than I recall?' he thought to himself.

Their eyes met and her cheeks flushed pink.

"This isn't what I expected, Nick," she whispered, her gaze going to his bare chest.

"Are you saying that you had some sort of expectation?" he stated with equal sincerity.

Her eyes darted to his, registering the change in green to gray combination. "I don't know," she started. "All I know is that last night, I didn't want to be anywhere else but right here, in your arms, making love to you."

"That doesn't answer my question."

Nodding once, she knew the usual deflection tactic was winning. "The minute I got out of Devin's car, the first thing I did was look in this direction; to this house, to where I knew a part of you still remained."

"Old habits," he baited quietly.

"Maybe, but you're married, so it doesn't matter."

His brow furrowed together, his body lifting to his elbows as he gave her the gravest of glares. "Why do you always fall back on that phrase?" he asked.

As if being scolded, Maggie sat straighter, her arms folding in front of her to cover her bare chest. "Are you going to sit there, after all these years, and tell me that marriage means nothing to you?"

"And will you ever out right answer a question I ask?" he responded with equal frankness.

They both stared at each other, contemplating a response that neither wanted to give. An argument was futile. It would gain them nothing.

Nicholas couldn't get past the fact that if he had to have her anywhere, it would be right there in that bed.

And Maggie recalled arguing with Nicholas caused more heartache than satisfaction in the long run.

"I don't want to fight," she whispered, hoping the change in her demeanor would bring him back to the place they'd found last night.

"I never wanted to fight with you," he returned, pulling her to come crashing onto his chest. His mouth captured hers, sending them into a realm of un-satiated desire.

It was a new day, one which took them back to a time when life was theirs, love was theirs, and the future was theirs.

Much later that day, Nicholas lent Maggie his sweat pants and a t-shirt to make the short trip across the street. They left the warmth and comfort of his bedroom, curious if they would meet any wandering eyes, but they didn't.

"Do you want me to walk you across the street?"

She shook her head, "I'm good. Just promise me you won't ignore me tonight when I'm sitting across the lawn from you."

"I think it's safe to say no part of me is capable of ignoring you at this point, Mags."

"I wouldn't know, it has been a decade."

"Yes, indeed it has," he replied, sliding the palm of his hand from her waist down to her butt, smacking it once, the sting causing her to giggle at his forwardness.

She leaned forward just as he opened the front door and she planted a firm kiss on his closed lips.

Leaving him standing there, Maggie walked across the street, taking in the afternoon heat as her feet quickened to her grandmothers yard.

There was no way of knowing how Consuela would react to Maggie's absence, so she walked into the house plain faced and vocal to her arrival.

"Abuelita?" she called out.

When she didn't respond immediately, Maggie went looking for her. She wasn't inside the house. Not thinking anything of it, she went to her room and quickly changed out of Nicholas' clothes.

Deciding the room was too dark, she began to open the blinds in her room. That was when she realized where Abuelita had gone. She was out in the back yard swinging on the hammock between the two far orange trees.

She looked divinely comfortable.

Missing her more than ever, Maggie left the quiet space and ventured out into her grandmother's backyard.

Just as she reached the hammock, Consuela shifted her body on the hammock and grabbed both sides.

"Hi," she offered her granddaughter.

"Do you mind some company?" Maggie asked, taking hold of the hammocks edge.

"Be my guest, just don't flip us." Her warning came with a sense of lighthearted fun, but Maggie could tell that her grandmother wouldn't be well off if she took a fall from the height of the netted rocker.

Carefully and with grace, Maggie joined her grandmother.

They spent several minutes rocking in silence, taking in the late spring air. The continued heat signaling summer was just around the corner.

"When I fell in love with your grandfather," Consuela spoke quietly, giving Maggie a sideways glance, "my whole world stopped for him."

"I fell so completely for him, that I felt happiness the most paramount of all things. That without him, I would suffocate. You can imagine how devastated I was when we had our first argument," she smiled, secretly recalling the aftermath.

"It took me years to realize that love endures all things if you are willing to be true to it. Eventually, I too began to wait for the other shoe to fall, never trusting the longevity of bliss."

Her hand found Maggie's and tenderly she squeezed it, for what she was about to say needed to sink in.

"From the moment, I realized how deeply in love with him I was, until the very day he died. I waited but it never came, my dear. Not until he was no longer of this life."

"I don't understand," Maggie stated questioningly.

"You see, even in the darkest moments of our love, I was happy because I was unhappy with him. We were together, committed to each other, because together we were one. We would never be who we were meant to be if we were apart."

"You should have been a writer Abuelita. My publisher would devour your quotes," she teased light heartedly.

"You found each other again last night. Don't waste this second chance," she advised, clearing the air in her own unique manner.

"How can I know that this is truly a second chance? He's married, and that isn't just circumstantial. It's fact."

"Have you cleared the air about his situation?"

Of course they hadn't. They were too busy last night devouring each other and falling into old habits.

"We didn't talk much," she giggled, becoming amused when Abuelita giggled with her.

"Just make sure you don't repeat old mistakes, Mi-ha."

"Oh, you mean Wesley. Yes, well, he is an issue isn't he?" I teased.

"Mira, you need to be clear with him where you stand. Melanie is more in love with him now than she ever was as a child. I've seen the change in him instantly and I'm sure so did Nicholas. He will always have a place in your life but that does not define a relationship, or a friendship."

"I understand, but how do I make them understand?" Maggie sighed, struggling with the challenge ahead of her. "How do I make Melanie and Nicholas accept that I feel nothing more than platonic love for Wesley, and him, how do I get him to accept that I will only ever be capable of feeling just that?"

"Your actions, my love, your actions," she repeated, nodding to herself that all Maggie had to do was behave in the manner that expressed her emotions.

"That's easier said than done, Abuelita."

Melanie burst out into the back yard, her expression completely distraught. "I just had the worst lunch ever!" she cried out as she reached them, her body somehow making itself onto the hammock without toppling Consuela and Maggie.

14 SUCH PRIVATE THINGS
Maggie

July 2004

Nicholas and I spent an entire month blissfully unaware of our surroundings. We stayed in a bubble like state and got to know each other again.

I took Nick's concerns about his place in my life into consideration and made a clear effort to show him that he was who I loved, the most important person in my life.

Every now and then, Wesley would appear, make small talk with his best friend, but for just that month he didn't speak to me.

The statement I made to Devin about Nicholas and Wesley being the sun and moon in my life hung ever so delicate in my heart. I was forcing myself to live without the moon, and realized that eventually I would find it too difficult to breathe.

Abuelita found me one afternoon on the sofa, staring up at the ceiling fan, lost in thought.

"What's with this slumber state?"

My eyes darted to her and I saw the genuine concern lining her eyes. "I'm hot and tired. I don't want to go outside."

She lifted my bare feet and took a seat at the end of the golden floral sofa taking up most of the living room wall.

"Are you sick?" she asked plainly, her expression blank.

My eyes went back to the ceiling. "No, I don't think so."

"Margaret, you are 18 years old and you have a boyfriend, one who is very much older than you. I have to ask you this, even if you don't want to answer me," she said, the words making me move my head to face her.

"Could you be pregnant?"

My mouth fell open and a smile erupted across my face, "Abuelita, I'm a virgin. Nick and I have not had sex," I giggled at her.

While I'm sure she tried to hide her relief, I heard the breathe she released after I answered her.

"Bueno, if it isn't that, what is wrong with you. I have not seen you this melancholy since he was gone."

I wanted to avoid this conversation like one would avoid the plague but whom else better than Abuelita to bounce my growing rift with.

"It's Wesley. I miss him terrible and I'm not sure why."

She let out a huff and a laugh simultaneously, "maybe because he is your friend and we should not ignore our friends for the sake of our heart."

"But it is because of my heart that I need to stay away from him," I complained.

"Are you certain of that?"

No, I wasn't certain, but trying to find out could cause a blow out between all of us. Melanie, Nick, Wesley, and Myself.

"It's hot, why not call Wesley and ask him to go swimming. Like you always use to do in the summers. Have him call Nick, that way it's as if he is extending the olive branch. Show them both that being together doesn't mean you can't be something to both of them."

She had a point, one which I took into consideration as I wasted another hour watching the ceiling fan spin endlessly.

Courage bit me and I got up to make the call.

The phone rang several times before Wesley's voice came through the line.

"Hello?"

"Hey stranger," I tried to sound sweet, and hoped he took it that way.

"Mags," his tone clear and direct.

"You doing something?" knowing this could go one of two ways so being direct was my only option.

"Nope, you?"

"Call Nick and ask him for us to go swimming," It sounded bad….so very bad.

He let out a chuckle, the amusement obvious, "miss me, do you?"

"Wes, don't be an ass. Just call him," I sassed him, knowing his cocky nature could only get worse if I didn't make a stance.

"What's in it for me?" he boldly asked.

"Nothing, forget it. I thought this would be simple," I argued, feeling defeat looming over the phone call.

"No, fine. I'll call him. I'll see you in a little while." He changed his tone, hanging up before I could say anything more.

One minute I'm tied up in knots, the next I'm smiling and jumping, up and down like a foolish child.

The phone rang and all I could do was stare at it. It was Nick. It had to be.

"Hello?" I picked it up, doing my best to control the butterflies swarming my stomach.

"Let's go swimming," he suggested, a smile evident in his voice. Could it be he was missing his friend as well?

"Uh, sure, give me a minute to change and I will be out."

Now, so long as Wesley kept his mouth shut as to whose idea it was, everything would be alright.

Twenty minutes later Nicholas and I were walking through the privacy fence that lead into Wesley's back yard. He was already in the pool, and I noticed that he was already drinking a beer.

"Isn't it a little early for that?" I asked, realizing how much like a nag I sounded.

He didn't respond, merely threw me a dagger glare and pushed himself deeper into the pool.

"How have you been man? I haven't seen you around much," Nicholas asked him and they greeted each other.

I listened, staying at the edge with my feet inching slowly into the water. To think, only an hour ago I had been worried their friendship was suffering because of me, and here we all were as if time had not tarnished it a bit.

"So are you going to come in?" Wesley asked me, his eyes focused on my legs.

"Yeah, babe, jump in. It feels great," Nick encouraged.

I merely shook my head at them, "when have you ever known me to just jump in?"

They turned to each other and burst out into laughter, as if recalling something that I didn't know.

"What?" I asked, sheepishly aware that they were laughing at me.

"Oh, I don't know, maybe because when you were little you use to jump in all the time with Wesley and I," Nick chuckled at the memory.

How was it that I couldn't quite remember it that way? I remember ogling at them and Melanie jumping in to show them that she wasn't scared of the deep end.

"That was Mel, that wasn't me."

"Oh, it was you my friend. I even have pictures to prove it," Wesley assured me.

"What pictures?" I asked, shocked that I was oblivious to this.

"Marcy took pictures of us one weekend for a scrap book she was making of Carmen Street memories. She said she wanted some of us to show the newer generation were as much family as previous generations."

"I had no idea," my voice trailed off.

As I sat there on the edge of the pool, I found myself staring at how Wesley's blue eyes sparkled against the glare of the water and how the water dripped off his shoulders and chest. When I realized what I was doing, I shot a look at Nicholas, who was completely aware of where my attentions laid.

Deflection was a must, "I am not afraid of the water."

"Then come in," Nick urged, his arms reaching out for me.

That was all it took for me to reach down to the hem of my shirt and pull it over my head. My sight fell to my bare skin, and the worry of how I looked ever present in my inability to accept being so under dressed.

I jumped in the pool and swam into Nicholas' arms. The heat of his skin soothing every nerve ending. His mouth reached my ear, "you are beautiful, my love," he whispered so that only I could hear.

I laid my head on his shoulder and let him swim us around. He continued his conversation with Wesley, but didn't let go.

Every now and again I would catch Wesley's eyes on me as they spoke, but Nicholas never acknowledged the looks.

We left feeling refreshed, not just of the skin but also of the soul. Making it to the edge of my driveway before saying anything, "I talked to Devin the other day, Maggie," he said, his words stopping my feet.

"Oh," I sighed softly, wondering what they had to talk about.

"Maybe it was wrong of him but he told me what you said about Wesley and me."

My eyes slightly widened at the embarrassment of being ousted by my own brother.

"I wish he hadn't done that," I admitted gravely, thinking of how it was a betrayal of trust.

"He had good reason to tell me, and I appreciate his words, even if a part of me is hurt by the truth."

"I never wanted you to be hurt, which is why I said nothing," I tried to assure him.

His hand reached out to me, and I took it. "I want to be both your sun and your moon but I can't change the fact that I was gone for such a long time. Wesley means a lot to both of us and I am willing to make this work."

This was the olive branch, this was how love works. Abuelita was right when she said that love finds a way.

"I want to make this work too," I agreed with his sentiment.

"There is something else," he added.

My eyebrow rose in interest to the tone in his voice.

"I want you to be mine in all ways, Magpie. I don't want to pressure you and we've never talked about it. Plus, I have to admit, seeing you today wearing nothing more than that little bikini, has me hot for you."

"It could be this heat," I teased, closing the distance between us, placing my arms around his shoulders so that our bodies touched.

"It's you, I can assure you," he insisted, his hands sliding down my back to push my nether regions up against the obvious fact to which he was referring.

"Well then," I said, staring at his lips. "I think we can have the discussion now."

"Tonight?" he asked, his need throbbing against my skin.

Nerves jumbled and anticipation grew, but I couldn't quite say yes.

What is wrong with you Margaret? I asked myself, my body tensing.

"Seriously?" he asked, the quick change in his temperament startling me.

He let go of me and took a step back, his eyes now filling with pain instead of an increasing desire.

"What?" was all I could summon mouth to respond.

"Is this about him? Is he the reason you won't submit to me? To give yourself to me? I mean, he has already ruined all matters of the heart," his voice was raised, making me flush in embarrassment.

"Wait, don't bring him into this," I shot back, my limbs finding their own strength to stand confidently in front of him.

"You don't get it do you?" he asked. "I am in love with you and want you to love me back with the same intensity. For Christ's sakes, Maggie, I could have had any girl of my choosing ages ago, but no, I waited for you. I've been waiting for you!" the pain was clear in his voice.

"You are taking this all wrong. I'm not hesitating because of anything other than the fact that you will be my first Nick. Does that mean anything to you?" I yelled at him, looking around to see if anyone was outside to hear me admit such a private thing.

Instantly his demeanor changed, the look on his face went from pain to defeat.

"I...I..." he tried to say.

"I do want to, I'm just afraid," I admitted quietly, moving forward to be close to him.

He wrapped me gently in his arms and softly whispered "I'm sorry, Maggie. I guess I wasn't thinking."

15 REUNION

June 2015

Maggie and Consuela focused on Melanie's protest and angst about her lunch. She'd run into Dominic while at lunch with Alyssa. She'd asked Dominic to join them seeing as how the lunch with Alyssa was meant to iron out details for the get together.

"He sat down, listened to all of the details, and got in a huff when I told him that Nash and Daphne had just confirmed this morning they would be coming. His reaction was completely unlike him." She paused, obviously shaken, "It was horrible."

Consuela remembered Dominic's generation drama, and had all but pushed it into a memory drawer. It was not unlike Dominic to react harshly to hearing Nash and Daphne's name strung together in the same sentence.

Melanie grasped Maggie's hands in her own, "Please tell me you will have Devin talk to him. Tonight needs to go off without a hitch."

"I will talk to him but I think this goes beyond the bounds of what Devin, the 'all-mighty peacemaker' can make right," she teased her. "And why does it need to be perfect, this isn't but a reunion of sorts, Mel."

"Devin won't be able to fix Dominic's problem, girls. It's something that has nothing to do with him." Consuela added, making herself comfortable again in the hammock.

"What is that suppose to mean?" Melanie asked, getting up and standing to face them. The tone of concern ever present.

"It means, my dear, that Nash, Daphne, and Dominic's issue is one of the heart. No one can make the heart want something that it doesn't. It wants what it wants. Devin is better off minding his own business," she said, her eyes closing, a need of rest becoming clear to the girls.

Maggie kissed her grandmother on the forehead, "Thank you Abuelita."

She nodded her head and sleep quickly took her for an afternoon siesta.

Maggie got up from the hammock and looped her arm through Melanie's as they walked back to the house.

"So what does Alyssa have to say?" Maggie asked Melanie, making it a point to calm her cousin down enough to have a decent conversation.

"Nothing really, she's just crazy busy. She is excited to see you tonight."

Alyssa had been like a fairy god mother for the two girls in their teenage years. They'd always looked up to her, even now.

"I will be glad to see her, it's been too long." Maggie sighed, closing the door of the house behind her as Melanie walked through the laundry room and in to the living room.

"What do you think happened between Dominic and the others to create such a rift?" Melanie asked, appreciating that Maggie was the one with the imagination.

"It could have been a lot of things, but what good does it do to make assumptions?"

Melanie nodded, "No, you're right. I just wonder if it has anything to do with a love triangle." She was making the connection to bring the subject up about their own situation.

"I wouldn't know." Maggie replied, not wanting to play into Melanie's game.

"Look, let me just flat out tell you. I plan on asking Wesley to be together tonight. Now that I know the whole truth about your history I feel I can take in the whole picture better, be more objective. I just don't want anything to go wrong.

"Anything, as in, me getting in the way of that?" Maggie bluntly finished.

"I suppose you could put it that way."

"Oh believe me when I say, Wesley is not on my agenda Mel."

"What is that suppose to mean?"

Maggie's cheeks flushed at the memory of how she'd woken in Nicholas' arms that very morning.

"I spent the night with Nick last night."

Melanie jumped out of her seat, "What?" she shouted, a smile spreading across her face signaling enjoyment and not judgment.

"I wasn't going to say anything, we can't have this be public knowledge. I don't want his issues to get worse because of our involvement."

"He is getting a divorce Mags, his relationship is all but severed with her."

"But it's not final, and I'm not going to make any assumptions as to what last night means for us."

Melanie went to sit next to her cousin, "You are foolish to think that last night meant nothing to him. He has been in love with you for as long as I can remember."

"And I remember a time where he loathed me."

"Well you know what they say about the fine line between love and hate."

"What, that they can get blurry sometimes?"

Maggie's cell phone started buzzing, the jolt causing her to jump in surprise. The two burst into a frenzy of giggles as she took it out of her pocket and realized who it was calling.

"I have to take this call, excuse me," she asked Mel as she left to the living room and briskly walked to her room before answering the call.

"Hello, hello?" She heard the male voice on the other side say several times.

"Is there something wrong? I asked you to wait until I called you unless there was an emergency," she scolded him, her hushed tone making it clear that she couldn't talk freely.

"I need the files. You didn't leave me the information," he urged her.

"Fine, give me an hour and I will forward them. Please send my love and I will talk to you soon." With that she hung up, knowing the probability of Melanie eavesdropping was greater than ever before.

She pressed end and stared at her iPhone screen. Her whole

life is back at home, in Chicago, and here she stood in the one place she had been running from for the past decade.

A soft knock on her bedroom door return her thoughts to what the day held in store for both Melanie and herself. A reunion, with everyone she'd grown up with. A Carmen street get together like the ones Abuelita use to throw when Maggie was a kid.

"Come in." Maggie replied.

Melanie opened the door and poke in to see her. "You okay?"

Maggie nodded but took a seat on the edge of the bed. "Have you ever wondered about where you would be if things had been different growing up?"

"Are we talking about me, or you?" Melanie teased.

"In general, does the thought ever cross your mind?"

"You mean like, if I had made a different choice in my life if it would have taken a different path, type thing?" she played along.

"Yeah."

"I think everyone has done that at one point or another, Mags," she paused. "But your life is great, why would you ever ask yourself that, because of Nick?"

"I suppose," Maggie answered, her gaze wandering to the

window that faced the back yard, to see Abuelita still on the hammock.

"Maybe life is giving you a second chance." Melanie placed her hand on Maggie's and she patted it.

Three hours later, Melanie was helping Devin set up tables and chairs out front of Consuela's house. Barbara was inside helping with the final touches on the meal, and even Scarlet was over helping with the set up.

"Where is your wife, Devin?" Scarlet asked, her curiosity peeking Maggie's interest.

Her body straighten at the question and she watched as Devin slowed in his movements, noticing as he thought about his response before replying, "she isn't feeling well, so she decided to stay home."

"I'm sorry to hear that. I always enjoy her company at these little get-togethers."

He nodded, not lifting his head to look at her, merely moving on to the next set of tables that needed unfolding.

Scarlet found Maggie staring at her with a grin spread across from ear to ear, "Hi there," she giggled.

"Hi there to you too sexy. What is this I hear about your walk of shame this morning?" she replied with a giggle of her own.

Maggie's eyes widened, turning as Scarlet passed her to walk towards the porch walkway.

"Who told you that?" she asked in a hushed tone.

"Well you know how things travel like wildfire in this neighborhood. I can't imagine I would want anyone knowing my whereabouts if I was a famous writer either."

"Shit, the press would have a field day with it being the content of my last novel was a little dirtier for the wary."

"How can it get any dirtier, Mags?" they both erupted in full blown laughter.

Consuela walked out to where they stood, made a quick survey of Devin's progress and sighed, "I think we are going to need more help."

"I can go ask around?" Maggie offered, her true intentions hidden behind the fact that she was itching to go see Nicholas.

"Do what you can, we need to start the fire-pit, and get the refreshments put out," Consuela motioned before turning to go back into the kitchen.

Maggie and Scarlet turned to each other and finished the laugh. "I will go find Nicholas."

"And I will see if your brother needs any more help," Scarlet winked at Maggie.

The two set about their own tasks as Consuela watched to see where her grand-daughters feet would take her first.

 She was pleased when she found her running across Nicholas' front yard.

"What do you think about them apples, Consuela?" Barbara asked, standing next to her lifelong friend.

"I think, my dear, that love will prevail after all."

"But he doesn't know everything," Barbara warned.

"No, but the past and the present can't erase how much they care for one another." Consuela turned to face Barbara.

"Tonight is going to be a true reunion, isn't it?"

"I only wish Tom had been here to see it," Consuela stated sadly. Her eyes misting to the memory of how they had argued.

16 ROMANCING THE SUN
Maggie

Christmas 2004

I'd spent the better part of 5 months trying to convince Nicholas that I was ready to commit to a more romantic relationship. Well, forget using the phrase, 'more romantic', hell, I was looking to jump in head first.

After our initial start to the sex talk, he put a huge halt to the idea and put more of an emphasis to our emotional connection.

Sometimes I found myself wanting to strangle him. Seriously, I contemplated the idea, wondering if men get anything a woman is possibly going through.

The jury is out for now. I can't put my finger on what it is exactly that prevents him from understanding my point of view.

For example, today, when I stopped by his house to pick him up for a get together we planned on attending, he asked me to sit and watch the end of the race with him. I stared, dumbfounded that he didn't understand how wrong it was to come late to a dinner party.

"People come late all the time, babe."

"Yes, they do, and we hear people complain about them throughout the entire meal. It's rude."

"Yeah, but those people do it on purpose."

"I'm not, 'those people' Nick. I don't want Marcus and his girlfriend to go putting nasty comments in other's ears about us."

"So what if they talk, people will find anything to talk about you if they really want to."

I threw my arms up in the air for no amount of explaining would get him to lift his behind off the sofa to leave for the party.

Taking matters into my own crazy hands, because at that precise moment I was feeling the twinge of insanity going on, and reached over him to take the remote off the sofa.

Miscalculation has always been a fault. Leave it to me to reach and stumble, or reach and knock something over. In this case I managed to do both.

His arms wrapped around my midsection and he somehow

twisted me all the way around so that I was laying flat on the seat cushions of the sofa and he leaned directly over me. I could look straight up into his eyes, given the position he had me pinned.

"Why must you be so forceful?" he asked, his voice neither angry not overly playful.

In my peripheral vision I saw the remote laying right on the floor by me. Close enough that all I had to do was reach out and grab a hold of it.

Doing just that, "Why must you be so stubborn?" I asked as I tugged the remote behind my back.

The smile slowly spread across his face and I was worse for the wear being in no position to tease him.

"Give me the remote, Maggie," the warning in his voice filled with mischief.

I couldn't speak for fear that the giggle would erupt from my throat. I shook my head and held firmly to the remote snuggled under my back.

30 seconds...that was all it took. 30 seconds of tickling, screaming, laughing, and wiggling for him to get my hands from behind my back.

He did managed to get the remote and we were still late to the dinner party, but the smiles plastered across our faces did little to cause snickering, if anything there were slight whispers as to what we had been doing to make us late.

If Only!

Christmas was just around the corner, the one time of the year that Carmen Street literally felt alive. Each of the families, young and old, made it a point to put Christmas lights up on their house. Even the Jewish family added decorations of their own to celebrate their holiday.

Wesley's dad always over did it, but everyone enjoyed it, looked forward to see what he would add to his display each year.

Abuela planned for Noche Buena, which is Christmas Eve. Our family roasts a pig in a brick fireplace out in the back yard and we rock from sun up to sun down.

The kids that had grown up on the block were all adults now. We'd gone from stickball games, to tossing the football, to just sitting out in the front yards and catching up. The older generation had children of their own, that were trotting around, making everyone feel old.

This year, Melanie and I asked Wesley and Nick to spend the day with us rocking the pig. At first there was rift because their own families had things going on, but our pouted lips managed to do the trick.

"So 12 hours, huh?" Wesley asked Melanie, trying his hardest not to bring me into the conversation.

A big grin made her face gleam with amusement, "yep, 12 whole hours!" she squealed. Her excitement was incredible, like she had taken something.

"Mel, a little less coffee today," I mused.

Nicholas took my hand, "hey, I have to go do something. I'll be back in a little bit, okay."

I straightened in my chair as he walked away, leaving me there with Melanie and Wesley.

"Do you know what that is about?" I asked Wes.

"Not at all. Not to change the subject but have you decided anything about Brown yet?"

College, the one subject I honestly didn't want to discuss with anyone, especially Wesley.

I shook my head at him and turned to Melanie, "Do you know if Abuelita is done making the flan?"

"You are going to have to check, I'm sorry," she apologized, making the expression of being concerned that it wasn't even thought of.

"I'll be right back," I jumped out of my seat and headed back into the house, slowing at the gate to see if Nicholas' truck was still in the driveway of his house. It was.

"Hey, Abuelita, did you make the flans yet?" I called out as I walked into the kitchen, coming face to face with papa Tom.

"Oh, hello papa. How are you?" I asked, wrapping my arms around his old body.

"My sweet, I am so much better that I got to see you. How are you? Have you made arrangements to head off to New York?" he asked, his intentions as clear as a cloudless night.

"Papa, I need a little more time to make that decision. I don't want to just up and leave."

His eyebrows furrowed together, disapproval spreading through his expression. "This isn't something you can just say no to, Margaret." His use of my whole name signaling that I should change the subject, but I just couldn't.

"I don't want to leave Tampa to go to school."

"You are too good to go to the community college or even USF. This is Brown, Margaret. You know how many people dream of getting into a school like that?" and there it was. Disapproval at its core.

"I'm not saying I'm not going to go, I just need a little more time." As I said it, Nicholas walked into the kitchen from the carport.

Tom diverted his attention to him as he rounded the table and his whole body stiffened. "This is your fault. She wouldn't be twiddle fiddling around if you weren't pulling on her heart strings like you are. I swear, you are going to ruin her future son." Tom fussed at Nicholas before storming out of the kitchen and into the living room where Abuelita and Grandma Barbara were hanging out.

I could hear them asking him what all the fuss was about

141

but the damage had already been done. Nicholas was staring at me defeated and pushed out. The hurt was evident.

"Let's go for a walk," I suggested.

"Do you think that is the best thing to do?" he asked me plainly.

I nodded once, knowing just what I would do. Courage moving my limbs, and confidence filling my heart.

I took his hand in my own, led him through the kitchen door and out of the house. Leading the way, I took him to his driveway.

"My parents left," he warned me.

"Even better," I smiled a cat like smile.

Holding back for just a moment, he looked me over, almost as if second guessing my suggestion.

Squeezing my palm a little tighter, he led the rest of the way, stopping only to unlock the front door.

Just as the door latched closed, I pulled his body around towards me and brought him down for a kiss. Hard and needy he returned the kiss with a groan. The, 'Oh Yes, this is what I need' type of groan.

His hands wrapped around my waist and he pulled me tight against him. That was all it took to send me into a wanting frenzy. I didn't want to wait anymore. I needed him right then.

I pushed myself out of his arms and held my hand out between us. "You can't tell me we need to stop this no matter how long it takes," I warned him.

"Baby, I don't want to wait anymore either," he whispered, his eyes smoldering, filled with an evident need of his own.

He reached back out to me and took my hand, tugging me gently towards his bedroom.

He'd let me walk in first and locked the door behind him. The latch forcing me to turn around. His room was dark, curtains completely closed, only allowing a sliver of light to escape into the small space.

Suddenly, I knew, I didn't need light to romance the sun. He was enough to make everything bright.

His hands took hold of mine and he brought me back up against his rock hard body. Our mouths crushed together once more and I was lost in a rhythmic dance of pleasure. His hands slid up my thighs causing my dress to come up over my waist. The heat of his touch reached its limit as he brought his forefinger to gently rub the soft center of my panties. Up and down he tenderly rubbed my nub as his kiss became deeper, more passionate.

I heard myself inhale sharply as he slipped one finger under the thin lace that separated his hand from flesh.

It was such an intimate touch I felt I would melt just as I was.

"Mmmm, you are so wet," he sighed over my mouth.

My eyes fluttered open and I saw his desire.

Slowly and carefully he helped me out of my dress, laying soft sweet kisses on my skin as it became exposed.

Taking his lead, I reached down to his jeans, undid the belt and then the button. Our eyes met as I slowly, methodically unzipped them. Inch by inch I watched his eyes, the anticipation too great to bare.

It wasn't until he slid off his jeans and was as bare as he was when he came into this world that I quivered with a twinge of fear.

How is that suppose to fit inside of me? I thought to myself.

I could sense my eyes widen a little and my limbs become a bit tense.

"I will be gentle, I promise," he tried to assure me, but I couldn't get back to my courageous self until his mouth covered mine.

I got on to the bed and scooted myself to lay on one of the pillows. He laid next to me, his body resting on one of his elbows.

"Merry Christmas, Magpie."

I smiled at him and inwardly felt like the luckiest girl in the world. "Merry Christmas, Nicholas," I whispered before I reached up and kissed him again, this time thrusting my tongue into his mouth. His other hand went to my neck and held my head, not to break the kiss. I could feel his full erection laying on my thigh, which made me curious as to what grabbing it would do.

I caressed his thigh until I found his manhood and I took it fully in my hand. I felt him take in a sharp breath at my touch and he broke the kiss.

"Oh my God, Mags." I felt him quiver.

Feeling it was the right thing, I slowly rubbed the entire length of his shaft as his mouth crushed on mine until his whole body was moving with my movements. His hand went down to my wetness and he slowly slipped a finger into my most sensual of spots.

A moan escaped my mouth as he created a response that was fully controlled by my body.

He rubbed and stretched my sex with his finger as I slowly reached a heightened state of euphoria.

His body shifted from my side to directly over me. His erection lay at the opening of my sex. He kissed my neck and whispered into my ear that he would be as gentle as he could. With eyes on one another, he slowly pressed forward into me.

As he entered, I tensed with the pain. He stopped to let me take a deep breath and let the pain subside. I nodded, letting him know to continue. He pushed into me further until the full length of his shaft filled me and that feeling was amazing.

Slowly he pulled out, and gently thrust back into me. The more he did it, the better it felt, the closer to ecstasy I could feel myself getting. He buried his face into my neck as his need forced him to push farther and faster with each moment that passed.

I felt my limbs crash in a wave of incredible pleasure and I gave into my release. He too must have been feeling it because before I realized it, he was bucking and calling out my name. The heat of the room brought everything to come back to life.

His body fell next to mine and the only sound I could hear was the labored breathing from both of us.

17 OLD HABITS

June 2015

Maggie sat at a table very near Consuela's front porch and looked out at all the faces that showed up to the get together that evening. It was overwhelming, to say the least.

She was pleasantly surprised to notice Dominic had decided to sit next to Devin, which just happened to be the furthest seat away from Nash and Daphne.

Nicholas was off chatting with old friends, every so often catching Maggie's eye, making sure she was still in attendance.

A small part of him refused to take hold of the emotions that were coursing through his system. He was happy. Genuinely happy, more so than he had felt in a very long time, and it was because she was there, sitting as though she had never left.

The ruse of the whole situation is that he knew at some point she would up and proclaim the need to get back to her life back in Chicago.

Could he accept it? Her leaving again as she had so long ago. Something would have to give. The more he thought about it, he came to the same conclusion, she could write from anywhere. She was already an established author, no one would argue where she lived as long as she was still productive.

She caught him in thought and he tossed her another smile. Yes, he thought to himself, he was going to do whatever it took to make sure she stayed.

Melanie on the other hand was having a difficult time getting Wesley to remain attentive to her. There were far too many people in attendance for her to contend with old friends. She fell into the conversation frenzy with the girls and succumbed to the idea that Wesley was as distracted as a young boy.

Maggie couldn't help but people watch. It was part of her craft. Writers watch people, they let their imaginations ramble off into a fictitious world of what ifs and let the moments take them to places normal people could never understand.

Maybe it was the over abundance of wine, or the ambiance but Maggie could have sworn she saw Papa Tom walking on the out skirts of Jeremy's yard.

She got up, as if in a trance, unnoticed by the crowd, even though they surrounded her. Her feet taking her to the shadows that played tricks on her eyes.

The cool night air, away from the crowd, was casually waking her from the daydream of seeing him.

"Hello?" she called out into the night.

But nothing was out there, only a wanting to make amends with a phantom.

The ground crunched behind her and she turned, startled that she hadn't heard anyone earlier.

It was Wesley coming up behind her, "I'm sorry, I didn't mean to startle you."

"Jesus, Wes, you never learn do you?" she scolded him, her heart beating a little heavier than before.

"Old habits die hard, I suppose."

She shook her head and clasped her chest, the feeling taking longer to subside.

"What are you doing over here? I saw you walking past the fence but you didn't stop, you just kept going.

"I thought I saw something," she admitted sheepishly.

"Ghosts, my dear. I thought we settled it a long time ago

that there are no such things as ghosts.

"No, you scared the shit out of me pretending to be said ghost for a week straight until I finally caught you in the act," she scolded, smacking him at the memory of the horrid ordeal.

A part of him loved teasing her, it never felt like teasing a sister, something his mother had insisted upon him when things had started building between the two of them.

It was always a need to get under her skin, a need to be her main focal point, period.

Wesley chuckled, and pulled her in to a hug. "I'm sorry, for scaring you," he patted her back and then gently pushed her away.

Quickly changing the subject, not wanting to make light of the connection, "so are you planning on doing something about this torrid affair with Melanie?" she asked him.

"How do you know about that?" he blurted out without qualms of who might be hearing.

Maggie looked around, catching Nicholas' firm glare but didn't defer from continuing the conversation.

"I didn't, you just admitted it to me on your own." She mused at getting the inside scoop, internally happy that his heart held stronger strings for her cousin than herself.

He kicked his feet at the ground, bashfully admitting his

doubts. "Awe, I don't know Mags. She has always been pretty shallow, you know. I'm not sure it would work out if I went all in."

"I think it's kinda gone passed that, Wes. And as far as her being shallow, I disagree. She has been in love with you since before I moved into the neighborhood."

"Well shit, Mags, that's basically her whole life."

Her eyes widened at him, "No shit, Wes. Wake up," she teased.

He became serious as she giggled, looking up to the sky.

"Mags," he said, the softness in his voice bringing her to attention, "you forgive me, don't you?"

Her heart ached for him. Standing there before her, heart wide open, and concerned about her.

"I forgave you the moment you let me go all those years ago."

"I didn't have a choice. You would have gone anyway. It was the right thing to do. You had your whole life ahead of you, what could I give you and…"

She reached out, touching his cheek with her hand, "Old habits do die hard, don't they. I was more to blame, Wes. It was my childish emotions that set us on that forward motion, my choices that caused everything."

"It took a lot for Nicholas to forgive me, but then Melanie made it better. She gave me the attention I had been giving you."

"I'm telling you, Wes. You would be stupid not to see her standing right in front of you."

"I'm not, and I do see her."

"It's just like old times, isn't it?" Nicholas stated plainly, startling the two of them to jump away from each other.

"Not quite, Nick." Wesley spoke firmly, a rise in temperament filling the air around them.

"No? It looks like it from where I was standing," he bit back, taking a step closer to Wesley.

"Man, this is not us anymore," Wesley shook his head. "We may have baggage, but she isn't a toy we fight over. She never was," he finished, turning on his heels to head home.

Maggie's cheeks flush with embarrassment about being spoken of with such emotion.

Nick turned to her and didn't know what to say. He could argue, but what he was feeling had more to do with baseless jealousy and nothing to do with what was really going on inside.

"Tell me what's wrong?" She asked him before he could turn to leave.

A part of him felt defeated. This rollercoaster he thought he'd gotten off of, up and down, was tiresome.

"My wife texted earlier, just before you came over here," he started, gauging her reaction before continuing but the blank stare was not helpful.

"She says that she has the divorce papers and will sign them if I give her one good reason it will never work between us."

Maggie shook her head, the idea crazy of not wanting to fight for your marriage. "What did you say?"

"You see, I was ready to tell her that my heart has always belonged to someone else. Since I was a teenager, I'd been in love with this long legged brunette vixen that grew up in my neighborhood. I almost told her that she should just sign them to free me from a hell I hadn't contemplated the true depths of, but then I looked up and saw you talking to Wesley."

"So?" Maggie shot back far too quickly for her own good.

"So? He repeated questioningly. "So, I have been living in a hell the moment you left, since you betrayed me. I thought I could love you enough to forgive you but then I look up and you are next to him, like a moth to a flame.

"No, not like a moth to a flame, like a sister to a brother, like a friend who needs counsel, like any other person I grew up with."

"You didn't have sex with them though, Maggie, you had

sex with him. With Wesley. With my best friend. The one person I loved as much as I love you."

"I'm sorry, Nick, I'm sorry. What do you want me to say? I can't change the past. I'm trying to make it right. I'm here, standing in front of you asking you to tell me what I can do to make it right."

Nicholas just stared at her, there was nothing she could do.

"Go home, Margaret. I was wrong to think I could ever love you the way I did once."

She shoved at his shoulders, "Your wrong and you know it. You're just scared. Scared like the night I told you about the sun and the moon. You became both to me, and you were afraid I was lying. God damn it, Nick, I wasn't lying. I'm not lying. Every character, every love I write about is us. The severity, the all consuming need, it's us."

He closed the distance between them, taking her forearms into his grasp, "It's not us, us died the moment you left."

"I had to leave, I had to go or I would have lost everything. Tom may have been a bastard about many things but I survived because of his ultimatum. I became who I am because of the choice he gave me. You couldn't have done that for me, you wouldn't have, and you know it."

"All I know, Maggie, is that you didn't give me a chance to forgive you. You gave in and ran away. Taking everything with you and every chance of my future with you."

She stood there, awestruck by his confession. Had he felt this way ten years ago? Why hadn't he said anything before?

18 TATTOO
Maggie

February 2005

I've always disliked Valentine's Day, and don't get me wrong, the sentiment is not coming from any sort of bitter place in my personality make up. I've never agreed with an extra holiday in the year which caused our depression enriched society to reach maximum sadness levels all because they don't have a better half to share, I love you's with that day.

It's become too commercialized and the root of wanting relationships to have an excuse to share their emotional connection to one another. Has it ever occurred to anyone that relationships shouldn't be just about showing affection on one particular day in the year?

Hmmmm, maybe more people would stay married if they put a little more effort into the other 364 days out of the year.

Devin, being the male role model in my life, had made it pretty clear to me that he has no clue how to keep his relationship status stable. He tells me regularly that love isn't roses and daisies all the time and there is no such thing as greener pastures on the other side. It's a complexity people fall back on when they want out.

"Lest we never forget what Mom use to say, "you must tend to your own grass to make sure it keeps growing.'" Rolling his eyes at me, we walked down the card aisle at Eckerd's drugstore.

"Buying her chocolate isn't going to mend broken fences, Dev," I teased, referring to his current break up.

"It could patch a few slats here and there." He tried, tried, being the operative word there. Yes, he was trying.

Something I gave him mad props for was most men whine and complain that something is wrong but fail to be a problem solver. Devin is a fixer, always has been. Sadly he isn't really good at it.

"What are you getting Nicholas?" he asked, probably making sure I didn't forget why I begged him to come along.

I took a card from the shelf, smiled at the picture of the monkey dancing on the front and waved it at Devin.

"That's not fair, girls have it too easy."

"We are getting tattoos tonight," I corrected, making it clear that there was nothing easy about the gift we were giving

157

each other this year.

His reaction, bug eyed and gaping mouth wasn't what I expected.

"You are actually going to go through with that?" gasping at words. "I thought you were being sarcastic when you suggested it." He reminded me of how it really came out.

"I was, he wasn't." I rolled my eyes, swatting at a stuffed animal hanging from the shelf. "He obviously didn't hear it in the tone of my voice."

"Serves you right, you are forever being sarcastic to that man."

The absurdity of his observation caused my lips to smack, the noise echoing in the almost empty store.

"Are we done here?"

His eyes shot down to his cart, filled with nonsense. All of which he was probably hoping to fix his issues with his girlfriend.

The card I'd picked up wasn't for Nicholas, it was for Wesley. He'd recently gotten into a huge fight with Melanie and they were not on speaking terms. While Melanie is my cousin and my allegiance should be towards family, in this case I felt bad for Wes.

Melanie can be an unreasonable person at times and their relationship was based on his giving her everything her little heart desired, and her boosting his ego. There is only so far a girl can boost her boyfriend's ego before it seems that she has the better end of the deal.

I signed the card and sealed it closed before Nicholas came over that night. I'd written Wesley's name on the outside, my curved letters and bubbly hearts plastered everywhere on the card envelope.

It was probably the very first thing Nicholas noticed when he walked into the kitchen of Abuelita's house.

"Melanie got Wesley a card?" he questioned, looking from the card propped up on the table back to read my face.

My eyebrows shot up, not immediately answering the question when he asked. His reaction was a simple tilt of the head and mouth piercing, both of which made me a little snippy.

"I felt bad," I admitted, not just to getting him the card, but also the reasoning. "He is alone on a day he thinks of as big and I'm sure he is kicking himself for not making the effort to fix their relationship."

"It's not your place to make him feel better, Mags," he said, emphasizing the word 'feel' in his statement.

My head just shook. I know it's not my place, shit, he isn't even my boyfriend, but damn it, he is my friend. Why can't friends do something to cheer each other up just because they are in their own relationship?

"I don't see what the problem is," I stated plainly.

"Because you don't see things like Wesley and I see them. You're you, and nothing applies to you. It's always well and good because it's you and you never stop to think about how others might take what you do."

"Wesley has been my friend since I was a little girl, just like…"

"Not like me, and sure as hell not like Melanie," he finished my sentence, correcting what he suspected I was going to argue.

"Well, no, but he still is my friend. I should be allowed to try to bring a smile to his face."

"Look, I don't want to argue," he stopped the conversation in its tracks. "We have to be there before 7. That was the time I made for our appointment."

Without saying anything, I walked passed him to the kitchen door, grasped the door knob firmly and left him standing in the house. I knew he would follow, I just had hoped it wouldn't be to see me run smack dab into Wesley's brooding chest.

If ever there was a bad time to be a klutz it would be now, and of course I wasn't selected for wishful thinking.

"Something things never get old," Wesley teased me as he pulled me off of him, taking my forearms into his grasp.

"I'm sorry. I didn't expect to see you," I admitted, turning back to see Nicholas standing right behind me.

"We have to get going, taking Mags to get her first official ink," he told him from behind me. Being sandwiched between their conversation was the only place I didn't want to be.

"Oh that's cool," Wesley mused, his head lowering to look at me.

"Oh, I have something for you," I thought, taking the opportunity to exit the undesired closeness.

I ran back into the house, leaving them to talk as I took the Valentine's Day card off the table.

Walking back out, I caught them nodding their heads and stopping their conversation as I came closer. I reached out, card in hand and waited as Wesley stared at it.

"What's this?" he asked me, looking from the card back to me.

"It's a card. I picked it up earlier when I was out with Devin," I admitted sheepishly.

His eyes shot from the card to Nicholas. His demeanor utterly calm and unchanging.

"You got me a card?" he asked me again, his amusement chiming in my ears as I nodded to him.

He rounded Nicholas, taking the card, and pulling me in to a tender embrace. "Thank you, sweetheart," he whispered into my ear.

Somewhere deep in my heart I wanted to cry. After hearing Nicholas, and now feeling Wesley's reaction, I knew how wrong it had been. So much so, that I didn't say a word during the car ride to the tattoo parlor in Ybor City. It wasn't until Nicholas parked and turned to face me that I had the courage to say anything.

"It's okay, Maggie. I know it came from a genuine place," he attempted to soothe over my concern.

I looked at him, into his beautiful eyes, now shining an emerald green, and burst into tears. My hands shot up to cover my face.

He reached out to me and pulled me close to him, his arms wrapping around my waist. He shushed me softly until I felt ridiculous.

"I'm sorry," I said into his chest, turning and shifting to lay my head on his shoulder.

"I know baby, it's okay."

"How is it okay, Nick? Not too long ago, I was admitting to you how I felt about the two of you in my life, and then I go and show those emotions clear as day in a way I don't even realize can be misconstrued."

"Fine. You win. He is the moon in your life, but so what. I

am the sun. I am everything. Your words," he said, pulling me away far enough to be forced to look up at him. "You are both the sun and the moon in my life, always and forever. That is all that matters, and it does matter."

He'd gone and turned my phrase around and used it against me, about me, to explain one key detail about the love he felt for me. It was enough because we were enough.

We walked into the tattoo parlor and both got a sun and moon tattoo and while they each represented something different, they both meant we loved each other.

19 THE WORDS

June 2015

Nicholas let go of her arms and stood mere inches in front of her. The music and laughs in the background making it clear that no one had heard the words that came out of his mouth.

"Time doesn't heal all things, does it?" she asked him, the sadness ever-present in the words.

"I tried, Maggie. I tried to open up to you..."

"Tried?" she shot back, her arms shooting out from her sides. "It's only been a few days, for Christ's sakes."

While she had a point, and Nicholas inwardly accepted it, she would never know how he had imagined their second chance would play out. He'd secretly fantasized about their reunion, which was now turning out to be a total disaster

"A few days isn't going to change certain facts," he stated plainly. His statement raised a few red flags that she tried to hide unsuccessfully.

He'd seen the flicker in her eye, the tensing of her jaw line. "I know about your big secret Maggie. I know about Olivia."

He watched as her eyes slowly closed, and a tear lightly fell. Her body softened in submission, as if years of keeping such a tight hold on a secret had miraculously been lifted off her shoulders.

"How did you..." she started, and then stopped when her voice cracked on the words.

"Does it matter?" he asked, throwing her phrase back in her face, realizing, only after he'd said it, that it was probably the worst response given the situation.

"Yeah, actually it does," she bit back, the momma bear side of her taking front seat.

"I've known since she was two, Mags. I flew to New York, thinking that maybe I could bring you home. The idea that enough time had passed and you'd gotten homesick enough to change your mind about Brown. I didn't expect to find a toddler dictating what your dinner plans were going to consist of."

Maggie stood immobile, her heart pounding in her chest. He'd known for 7 whole years that she was a mother, that she'd never come back home because the proof was in her baggage.

"Cat get your tongue?" he tried to lighten the mood.

What is there to say? She thought to herself, knowing that what would come out of her mouth next could potentially end any hope either of them had for a future.

"The moment Livy was born, everything stopped being about everyone else, and started being about her. I wasn't ever going to come home to you or to Wesley out of love for either of you. I knew I had to base decisions of the heart on what would be best for her. I became a mother at the same time my heart had been shattered into a thousand pieces. So, yeah, maybe a cat did catch my tongue. Maybe I don't know how to have a conversation about someone who is everything to me with someone who once meant the same thing to me."

Consuela startled the two of them by clearing her throat and walking in to the streetlamp light shining just off to their side. "Y esto? What are you two doing over here?" she asked, her voice lined with concern at seeing Maggie's face flush with emotion.

"Nick was just telling me about his trip to New York, what did you say, 7 years ago?" she asked, "when he found out I have a daughter and didn't mention a word of it to me this whole time," she finished, feeling foolish.

"Me?" he shouted, astonished, "I didn't have to say anything. The real question here is if Wesley knows, because I sure as hell never asked him."

Consuela raised both of her hands at the two of them, quite annoyed that they sounded like arguing children, rather than adults trying to sort out a long history of mistakes.

"This is not the time or the place to be talking about such a delicate matter. The two of you need to go somewhere private if you want to work this out, but your neighbor's front yard, during a party, isn't the time or the place," Consuela scolded, taking her granddaughters arm and his, scooting them towards his parent's house.

Following command, they walked the distance across the street, only pausing on the porch to see Consuela staring at them as they walked fully out of sight and sound.

"She has a point. I've kept this to myself for so many years because of the gossip and nastiness that the talk does to our families. They've gone through enough as it is."

"That is absurd. Eventually things die down and the talk cycles to something else," he argued.

"Yeah, something else, until it cycles back to you. My daughter doesn't need to be the epicenter of ridicule and disrespect. It's not her fault what happened and I refuse to let anyone put her down because of it."

"And who would do that? Because my family wouldn't, Maggie, and you know that."

"No, but Wesley's family would. Marcy has had it out for me

since that summer we were caught playing man hunt in their back yard. She assumed such terrible things about me, so much so that I grew to hate it when she came over."

"She is just like that. You can't change people, Mags."

"No, but I can change myself. And that is exactly what I did. Can you imagine what the press would do if they realized that Olivia came from a torrid love affair and not from my child hood sweetheart. Because I will tell you, they all assume she is yours, even though they have never printed it."

"How do they know about me?" he shot back, amused that he'd been brought up at all in the same sentence with the press.

"They know because I told them about my childhood during an early interview in my career. After a while I stopped getting questioned about myself and more about my work, I was no longer the novelty everyone needed to unmask."

"Boy were they wrong."

"That isn't funny Nick. And Wesley does know. He is the one that encouraged me to go to Brown and accept Tom's ultimatum. To make something of myself, to be someone our daughter would look up to and admire."

"Why would he do that? She needs a father," his eyes wide with confusion."

"Because he stopped thinking about himself, and what was

best for me...and thought only of our daughter and her future."

"So he knows all about her?" Nicholas asked, finding a seat on the living room sofa.

"And she knows him, they have a relationship," she followed his actions.

Nicholas sat, shell shocked. Not sure he could have made such a choice; such a sacrifice for Margaret.

"I made a lot of mistakes but my daughter and the choice to keep her and raise her on my own was not one of them." She sighed, looking down at the floor, too ashamed because she'd not admitted any of it before to him. "When we argued on the street that afternoon and Tom came outside, my whole world came undone."

"I was angry with you because you didn't think, Mags. It was thoughtless, and selfish. Both of you were. You took every happy memory of our love and tarnished it with one stupid moment."

He'd gotten up, the need to touch her face growing in the pit of his stomach. He sat next to her and swiped at the tears sliding down her cheek.

"It was one moment, one instance that I became confused about the love I felt for you and how different it was to the love I felt for Wesley. I tried to excuse it, for so long, tried for my daughter, but deep down, I'd always known how confused I'd been."

He sighed, taking her hand in his own. "A few days isn't going to be enough Maggie. Hell, I don't even know if a few months would make a difference. All I know is that I've waited 10 years to have you in my arms. To feel the way my heart beats when you are near, to know that everything will be okay because you are home."

"Why has it always been hard for us to get to where we always wanted to be?"

"We were there sweetie, a lot. It just never lasted. Life had other plans for us."

"Then what makes you think that it will work out this time?"

"I don't but I'd rather try and fail then spend one more minute missing you and not being able to love you openly."

"You love me?" she asked him, the question coming out as a meager whimper.

A grin appeared as he nodded, changing his features completely. "You are in my bones, Magpie."

She leaned forward and placed a gentle kiss on his lips, acknowledging that his words were enough. The truth had been set free and now all that was left was for the pieces to fall where they may.

20 WESLEY
Maggie

Relationships are possibly the most fragile thing known to man. Maybe because emotions are the fabric that hold two people together, and that fact alone is as delicate a situation as brain surgery. Or maybe it's because all the odds are against two people maintaining a consistent level of happiness for prolonged periods of time.

Whatever the case, know that Nicholas and I have learned the power that make-up sex has on our ability to deal with relationship crap. It is pretty incredible if you ask me.

I fell in love with Nicholas long before I knew that relationships required a lot of work to achieve any form of longevity. His essence had been engraved in my soul years longer than we'd even had carnal knowledge of one another. So we were bound to face issues with expectations if either of us expected it or not.

Abuelita insists that young love is a passing fancy, in which we end up comparing all other loves in our life. It's that one foundational love that got our hearts going. If that is the case with Nicholas and I, then I feel bad for the poor schmuck that comes after him.

Then there is Wesley. Poor ol' Wesley, that insists on partying out on the town more days out of the week than there are names for. The only issue I have ever had with it is when he dragged Nick out with him.

Is it possible that my own jealousy sneaks out when they are together? That is what Devin thinks, at least.

"Nicholas may be your boyfriend, but Wesley is like his brother. You can't get angry with Nick for having issues about your relationship with Wesley when you give him grief for wanting to have his own friendship with the guy," Devin tried to explain.

"It's not that I don't want them to be friends, Devin, it's that they go out and make dumb choices when they are drunk together."

"What are they doing that is so dangerous to your relationship?"

"Well the strippers, for one. I'm sorry but I don't want some nasty girl getting any form of money from my boyfriend. If he wants a chick to dance for him, I can do that myself thank you very much."

"I can't say anything about that, Mags. Far be it from me to try and say anything about strippers and dollar bills," he chuckled under his breath.

We were sitting outside on the porch chairs, basking in the wonderful summer heat.

"Speaking of the devil himself," Devin murmured under his breath, nodding once towards Wesley's figure walking across the street to Nicholas' house.

He hadn't seen us sitting on the porch. He looked like a man with a one track mind.

"What do you think has him all huffy about?" Devin mused.

Not knowing any better, I got up and let my curiosity get the better of me. "I'm not sure, I'll be right back. I don't think Nicholas is home anyway," my voice trailing off, the mental thoughts pushing words to escape my breathe.

Why would Wesley be going over to Nick's when he could obviously tell that he wasn't even home.

I knocked on the red front door, hearing raised voices coming from the other side.

With one sharp tug, Austin's large figure came into view.

"Oh, hi. I didn't know you were home," I gasped, startled to see him looking at me.

"Now is not a good time," his firm voice all but shutting me out. He went to close the door but I caught Wesley staring at me from the living room, my hand stopping the door from closing.

"Where is Nick?" I asked Austin, also directing the question to his best friend.

"He isn't here, Margaret," his voice deeper and more curt than before. His intention was to make me leave, I got that much, but for the life of me, I wanted to know why he was being so rude. He had never before shut me out so completely.

My hands came up to my hips and my eyebrows furrowed at him. A clear indication as any that I wasn't going to be bullied into leaving without hearing Nick was okay.

Funny thing, growing up with people, they tend to know your behavior and persistence well enough to think twice before assuming.

"He went to a job interview," he started, trailing off before adding, "in Atlanta."

'What?'

While the word itself hadn't escaped my lips, Wesley huffed in response, reacting the way I would have had it been anyone other than Austin to break the news to me.

"Uh, and he is coming home when?" I asked.

Wesley came into view, standing mere inches behind Austin

at this point. "No one knows, Mags. He hasn't told anyone anything," he retorted.

Dumbfounded, I didn't know what to think, much less what to say. You would assume, that when you are in a relationship, that you would tell the person you love that you are going for a job interview in a different state.

Wesley left the house, shoving past Austin and bumping against me to get out of there, mumbling all the way, "this shit is stupid, Best friend my ass."

I didn't wait around with Austin, I turned and followed Wesley into the street. "Wait a minute," I tried to stop him. "I don't understand."

The words sent him spinning around and stopping dead in his tracks. His figure towered over mine, his blue eyes sparkling in the afternoon sunlight. The grave look on his face worried me more than anything.

He shook his head after a moment of staring me down. "Understand......" he said sternly but the manner in which he said it didn't sound like he was referring to Nicholas at all.

Without another word he turned sharply and started heading towards his house. The muscles on his back flexing through his t-shirt.

I watched maybe two or three steps before I called out his name. "Wesley, finish what you were going to say," I demanded. The tone in my voice making me sound like a totally different person.

When he stopped, he didn't turn around. It was up to me to close the distance. I walked across the street to meet him where he now stood, and as I suspected, he was hurt by his friend's actions.

"Tell me what's wrong. Why are you so upset?"

Maybe I was mistaken for feeling I had the right to know what was making him upset but an undeniable urge overtook me to try to make him feel better. To calm him down.

Slowly, and undeniably breathtakingly dangerous, Wesley turned and closed the distance between us. His tall lean figure standing statuesque like in front of me, his stern expression frozen on his face, his gaze smoldering with a mixture of anger and hurt but something else lined his thoughts, his demeanor.

"Come have a drink with me by the pool, Mags," he whispered in my face.

There were all kinds of sirens going off in my mind. Big warning signs blinking, 'No, Run Away'. But did I listen? No, I never listen to the reason skipping about in this crazy beautiful mind of mine.

He grasped a hold of my hand and guided me back to his back yard, to the wooden bar out by the pool. I sat on one of the long lounge chairs and watched as he made something on the rocks. I didn't ask, I knew that whatever he concocted I wouldn't like anyway.

I looked up at the trees that sprawled out above his backyard and wondered if he had played on the branches as a child.

"You know I know practically nothing about your childhood here," I stated, paying close attention to the two glasses he was carrying back to where I sat.

"It was basically the same way you grew up, except I wasn't shy or afraid to be myself."

"I wasn't afraid to be myself," I snapped back, bringing the glass up to my nose to smell the contents.

"It's strong. Just sip it," he warned before adding, "and yes, you were. It took years to see you free yourself from that fear. I never had that. I was born here so the relationships I had with everyone became second nature."

Rolling my eyes at his statement, I took the first sip. AAcckk, it was strong.

"Geez, Wes. Could you make it any stronger?"

Ignoring my complaining, he took a quick swig of the contents in his glass and sat the crystal down on the little table that separated our two chairs. It was almost like he was challenging me to drink mine as he had his, but when my eyes fell on the brown liquid I could recall the heat it created on my tongue.

Eyes darting to his, I knew that he wouldn't open up on my terms, so I had to do something, follow his terms on this one.

Placing the crystal to my lips, I held my breath and took a gulp of the fiery fluid. While at first it set my chest ablaze, within moments I could feel the dull numb of the alcohol.

My head shook at him. "How can you drink that stuff?" I asked, vaguely realizing he was laughing at me.

"It makes everything fade away, Mags. Sometimes I just need it all to fade away," he admitted, the sound of his voice echoing low in my ears.

He lifted his glass, pointing it towards me for me to follow suit. He waited until mine chimed against his, "to the sun and the moon." His eyes glaring into mine as he downed the remaining bit of his drink in one gulp.

My senses froze in time. A proverbial tidal wave did me in. I was clearly shocked and all he could do was snicker.

"Oh, come on Maggie. You didn't think Nicholas wouldn't tell me, or that Devin wouldn't warn me?"

I shook my head, "No Wesley, I didn't think they would tell you one fraction of what that statement means. Especially since it was said so very long ago."

"Oh, I've known for quite some time now. It just didn't

bother me so much as it does at this very moment."

I took the drink and down it myself, listening to his words and not wanting to chew his head off. The glass made a clank sound as it hit hard against the table, but the noise merely had him on his feet, snatching both glasses and heading back to the bar to refill them.

He'd known, damn him for being such a jackal. He'd known and never said anything. When Nicholas got upset at Valentine's Day, could it have been because he had discussed it with Wesley and their conversation added to his fears?

I didn't think to say anything until he was sitting back down across from me, but by then he was on a mission to finish his drink before me.

"You are going to get drunk," I stated clearly.

"Maybe that's what I want. Maybe I need to forget everything for just one small moment." He slouched in his chair and closed his eyes. His face tilting to the sky. "Finish your drink," he said.

Smiling and shaking my head at him, I gulped down the rest, realizing how much less it stung the second time down.

Following suit, I laid back and closed my eyes. I could feel the alcohol kicking in. The swirl of consciousness something to marvel at.

"Are you going to Brown?" he asked plainly, making me

open my eyes to notice him staring at me attentively.

"I don't know," I answered, his question coming from left field. "Why do you ask?"

"If Nick leaves, and you leave, then all I have is Melanie, and God help me but she drives me nuts sometimes. I'm not sure how long it will last before I end up in a nut house" he teased, shifting in his seat to lean forward.

"Nick isn't leaving. I'm not sure what Austin is talking about. It doesn't make any sense."

Wesley got up, took my glass and walked back to the bar. "It makes perfect sense. If he was going for a job interview in Atlanta, he would make damn sure no one knew about it so they wouldn't talk him out of it."

"Nicholas wouldn't leave home, he has said time and time again that having gone to school in North Carolina was a huge mistake."

"Yeah, but that had everything to do with you and less to do with the fact that it was away."

"I don't know, Wesley, this just sounds like some bogus story."

"Whatever, maybe it's the drinks talking."

"I doubt it, you always did have a flare for the imagination and your stories."

"My stories. You are the one with the full paid scholarship to Brown University for your ability to write."

"Sure whatever, I had you to get it from."

"Uh-huh", he mused.

Handing me another drink, I shot him a toothy grin.

"Yeah, keep smiling. Your sassiness won't last long."

The drink wouldn't last long either and I noticed how it didn't sting anymore. Quite frankly, I felt blissfully aware of my surroundings.

Wesley went from sitting on his own chair to sitting at the end of my lounge chair. I had my feet in a criss-cross position which made it possible for us to sit perfectly apart without touching one another. But the more I drank, the less I cared about the line in which we had always danced.

Eventually, Wesley brought the bottle over to the table and poured as we talked. We stopped counting at 3.

"You have pretty lips, Maggie. Has anyone ever told you that?" he slurred cheerfully.

Looking at his lips I realized they had gone a little blurry.

"Oh, I need glasses," I blurted out, shocked at the observation.

"Yeah, vision is jacked up 20/20," he laughed, the sound echoing off the walls of the house.

My eyes widened. "Stop being so loud, someone will get mad and I will never hear the end of it," I warned.

"What? It's not like anyone is sleeping, it's the middle of the afternoon. And besides, who is going to get mad. You are an adult for Christ's sake."

We both laughed hysterically after that. First, because only old people sleep in the afternoon and even if they were sleeping, they probably couldn't hear us anyway. Secondly, because he was right, I am an adult now. It wasn't like I was sneaking out in the middle of the night.

"You really do have pretty lips, Maggie. Can I kiss them?" he asked boldly.

My inhibitions had evacuated my senses quite some time ago, back at glass 2 maybe.

The corner of my mouth lifted, the thought of how one little kiss wouldn't hurt anything. It was just Wesley after all.

Had he read my mind? I thought.

He was putting his drink on the table and reaching out to take mine. Handing it to him, I wondered what was happening, but my thoughts didn't register.

He got up, moved his legs on either side of the lounge chair, so he would be directly in front of me.

"Hi," he mused.

"Hi," I replied with equal amusement.

His eyes fell on my lips but he did not move. He sat there, and I wondered if we could sit there, in that position for the entire afternoon. Problem with something so absurd is the boredom that I'm usually overcome by at all random times.

My eyes fell on his lips, finally. Nothing like the lips I was accustomed to kissing. These were thin and masculine. I wondered if I would like how they felt.

The thought took a hold of me and I found myself leaning forward so that my lips grazed upon his.

At first he didn't move, or breathe for that matter. I felt the difference immediately, registered the heat from his face.

His hand came up to the back of my head and tangled in the loose locks of my hair. That was when he reacted. His mouth opened, causing mine to do the same. I felt the swarm of desire as all thought seized to exist in my mind. His touch, his hold on me, the way he caressed my breast and moved his hand ever lower, was the only reflection in my foggy mind. The alcohol shut everything else off.

Without a word, we let the moment take us, knowing deep down that if we didn't it would be gone. Lost in the shadows of what ifs and wonders.

21 MENDING THE FENCE

June 2015

Morning's after tend to be filled with emotions that tittle on wobbly ground. Nothing seems clear except the need to abandon your current intertwined position and run for the hills.

She woke for the second straight morning in Nicholas' arms. There was no denying that while their history was thick with destruction; their current standing paved a new road of satiated passion.

Taking in the sight of him sleeping would never get old. She used to watch Olivia sleep as a baby, calling it the 'watching syndrome'. It happened quite often over the years with Livy, but now she was doing it again.

Sadly she realized that her time was quickly coming to an end. She'd have to go home and leave his side. She would have to go, not just because she was missing her daughter like crazy, but because her publisher was waiting to hear back about a project he'd presented her before she'd left.

Not wanting to have an early morning conversation with him, Maggie quickly dressed and found her escape from the room without waking him. However, fleeing from the house unnoticed was a different story all together. At the end of the hallway, she'd heard a rustling in the kitchen, cups being clanked together, and the wonderful coffee smell in the air.

There was no room for hesitation, she'd known, at some point, their relationship was bound to surface, the truth bound to come out.

Clearing the hallway and walking into the bright open kitchen area, she'd come face to face with Nicholas' mother, Mirabel.

The startled jolt she made when she turned to see Maggie half dressed at the edge of the kitchen was a key indicator that she hadn't known Nicholas had company.

"Oh, my," she spoke softly, her hands flying up to her mouth, surly to cover the half scream she had been about let out.

Her reaction brought Maggie into the kitchen, to make sure that she was okay. "I'm so sorry, I didn't mean to startle you," she tried to explain.

She shook her head and flapped her hand at Maggie, "Don't

worry about it. I just hadn't realized, otherwise I would have waited."

Maggie's cheeks flushed red, recalling the many times they'd had coffee together because she'd spent the night. The memories brought smiles to both women's faces and they giggled quietly.

"It's nice to see you again, my dear. Would you like a cup? It's is almost done," Maribel invited.

It was one invitation that Maggie couldn't resist. "I would love a cup, thank you. I seem to be more tired as of late."

Maribel nodded her head, "Yes, well, emotions have a way of exhausting us when they are in overdrive. I am sorry about your grandfather. Did you have a chance to mend the fences with him?" Her question came with an opening to talk about other things pertaining to Tom.

"We were not on speaking terms for most of my time away. Life happened and our differences were great."

"That is sad to hear. I pray nothing like that ever happens to us. I'd miss my boys too much," she sighed, handing Maggie her coffee mug.

"Thank you," she replied, "How is Austin, by the way?"

The older woman smiled to herself, as if being privy to a secret no one was allowed to know. She was in fact pleased that Maggie was interested in their little world. The interaction made her feel like they were getting back on a bicycle for the first time since childhood.

"He is great, spends his time in Miami a lot for work, but he lives nearby with his wife and two children, Caroline and Jason," she said, pointing to a few pictures on the refrigerator door.

"Wow, two children," Maggie marveled. "To think he disliked children so much as a young man," she teased, causing Maribel to nod her head in agreement.

"He did, but things change. People change."

They sat quiet for a moment, drinking their coffee and feeling the peace of the morning, until another figure entered the kitchen. Nicholas walked in, ruffled hair signaling that he got out of bed and jumped to see if Maggie was still there or if she had bolted before he'd had a chance to talk to her. Seeing her there calmed him down from the panic he felt waking to an empty bed.

"Good morning handsome," his mother cheered, returning the hug that he was giving her.

"I see the party started without me per usual."

Maggie shook her head, "Early bird..." she started, not expecting him to remember but he surprised her but chiming in at, "...gets the worm."

They both nodded, silently finding their way to one another.

"I really do have to get going. I need to make a few phone

calls I've been putting off and they might cut my visit short."

"We can talk about it later can't we?" he asked her, hoping she wouldn't find an excuse to leave him out dry.

"That sounds nice. Why don't you stop by Abuelita's house around dinner, 5?"

He moved in to kiss her but Maggie turned her face so he could kiss her cheek. His mother made her uncomfortable, always had.

Their eyes met, his closeness an intimidation tactic, "Five o'clock."

She looked into his eyes, "don't be late."

Her tone sweet and sensual causing a reaction he hadn't been prepared for. He found his hands reaching out to her forearms and grasping them. He softly pulled her close to him so that he could smell the sweet floral scent on her cloths, "I may need it to be a long dinner," he whispered into her hair.

"Nicholas" she said, hitting his arm playfully, referring to his mother being just behind him at the kitchen counter.

Their eyes met, but she knew that the day would drag on tirelessly.

Fact of the matter was, the time didn't drag on for her. The moment she opened her grandmother's kitchen door she was greeted by the kitchen table that was filled with the females of the family.

Consuela had wanted to have a nice breakfast with all her granddaughters before Maggie left for Chicago. She knew her granddaughter well enough to know that at any moment she would be itching to go back to that little girl of hers.

Alyssa threw her hands up in the air, "Well it's about damn time. I haven't been to sleep lady. Let's get this thing going." It was her way of being grateful to see her cousin.

"Had I known everyone would be here, I wouldn't have…" she trailed off, making eye contact with Melanie.

"We all watched you make the walk of shame, Maggie. There is no need to make explanations. If I was waking up in those arms, I would be late to everything," Luna teased, her cheeks blushing.

The heat rushing to her cheeks, secretly excited that it was out in the open and she wouldn't have to hide it from anyone anymore.

"Thank goodness you are not one of those famous people that the paparazzi follow around waiting to uncover all your secrets, this little romance would have taken a life of its own. Considering," Melanie said sarcastically.

Maggie had been smiling up until Melanie spoke the word, 'Considering'. It was bad enough that she had secrets, but to make the implication for the rest of her family to wonder about was a totally different thing. She knew that Olivia would eventually need to be discussed, but Maggie wasn't ready for that, not yet at least.

It was Alyssa that caught on before any of the other ladies in the room, "What is it with you two? Always with something to say and no courage to say it," her tone clearly annoyed by the stand offish behavior between the two of them.

"We were like that growing up, remember, Alyssa?" Luna teased her cousin.

"No, I don't ever remember purposefully making you blush the way Melanie does to Maggie," she stated, slowly getting up from the table. "And another thing...we all know that Wesley meant something to Maggie too. The four of you had an undeniable connection from the beginning, so to be pissy with your cousin because of a boy, is just plain pathetic."

Melanie sat wide eyed and in shock that Alyssa, who had always been so very P.C. about everything, all but chewed her out, defending Maggie no less.

"Mira, girls, we are not here to argue. Alyssa, sit down. There is something I need to discuss with all of you, and I'm sure you are not going to like it," Consuela sighed.

Almost simultaneously, all the ladies sitting at the table had turned to look at their grandmother.

Consuela nodded, knowing what she was about to say was the hardest decision she had ever made, but it was the right one. "I have decided to move."

The gasp escaped each of their mouths and eyes widened at their grandmother's words.

"Where are you going?" Luna asked, her hand having reached her lips with her shock.

"I am moving near Maggie, in Chicago."

From Consuela to Maggie, their attention shifted, but this was the first Maggie had heard of her grandmother's decision.

"This isn't coming from me girls. I didn't know either."

"No, it wasn't from you exactly. It was from another in this family which makes my heart yearn."

She was forcing Maggie's hand, she was making it almost impossible for the truth not to come out at that precise moment.

"What are you talking about, Abuelita?" Melanie asked, her confusion reaching its max.

"She means my daughter," Maggie confessed, her eyes directed at her grandmother.

While the second wave of shock riveted through the table, Maggie couldn't help but shake her head at her grandmother. She'd known, somewhere deep down that Consuela had no intentions of moving to Chicago. It was all a ruse to get Maggie to admit the truth to her cousins. For the truth to come out period.

"What are you talking about?" Luna asked Maggie.

She turned her head towards the rest of them, "I left ten years ago pregnant with Wesley's baby. Tom gave me an ultimatum and I made the choice that took me as far away from here that I could get."

"Dear God, does Wesley know?" Melanie half yelled at her. This whole time she'd just assumed that Maggie had gotten an abortion.

Maggie turned to see the anguish in Melanie's face. "Yes, he has always known. He encouraged me to take the offer, said it was the best decision for our child."

"He let you go?" Alyssa chimed in, the sad look forcing Maggie to understand what they were all concerned about.

"He didn't let me go because he didn't want to be a father. He has a relationship with Olivia. He let me go because deep down he loved us too much to keep us here to face the ridicule and disgust. He knew that I could have a future in writing if only I had the education to back it and Tom was providing for us in a way that he could not."

"On my God, does Nicholas know of your daughter?" Luna asked, the worry cracking in her voice.

That was when the room became silent. They all waited for me to tell them if he knew or not, and while he'd known the truth for many years, I wondered if he could genuinely forgive me for keeping the secret from him.

The truth is something that can never be kept hidden from those we care about and their reaction was proof I should have been more open about my life and my heart.

22 ULTIMATUMS
Maggie

July 2005

The two little blue lines on the white pregnancy test stick was the last thing I'd ever expected to see. I was hoping my period was late due to the stress of outright lying to Nicholas for the past 2 months, but stress had nothing to do with it.

I felt the weight of the world as I sat on the front porch of Abuelita's house waiting to see Wesley's car pull into his drive. Sadly, it was Nicholas' truck that pulled in first.

I couldn't help but feel terrified that he would just realize that I was pregnant. Not that I was showing or anything, but because I couldn't be that good of a liar.

He got out and rounded the truck, waiting for me to jump from the seat and run across the street like I'd done so many times over the years.

It didn't happen. I stared at him, wanting so badly to be in his arms and tell him how much I loved him, but I couldn't. Not now, it would sound like the worst lie of all.

The worst part of it all is the fact that I do love him, I just made a terrible mistake in a weak moment with someone we both care for.

I watched as his head tilted and he'd finally made the decision to come to me. Every step he made was one I feared would be the last.

"What's wrong baby, still feel sick?" his words like shooting knives into my heart.

I shook my head, feeling the need to tell him, the truth on the tip of my tongue.

"What is it then?" he asked, just as he reached the edge of the porch.

That was when I noticed Wesley's car pull in the driveway a few houses down. My attention jumped towards the car and Nicholas turned to see what I was looking at.

"What's going on with you and Wesley, Mags?" he asked, his face still turned towards Wesley's house. Probably watching as he got out of the car and waved towards us.

How could I say anything? Every word would make matters worse, make the truth of what grew inside me something tarnished and shameful.

Nicholas turned to me as Wesley walked our way. I noticed his jaw line clenching and his muscles tightening on his arms as he held on to the porch post waiting for me to say something.

The only response I could conjure were tears to pool in my eyes. Surely saying more than any words I could express.

A shadow cast upon Nicholas' figure, his eyes slowly closing. "What did you do, Margaret?" he asked me, his tone dark and grave.

He didn't look at me again. He just stared down at the ground waiting for Wesley to make his way to us.

"Hey guys, what's up?" he asked innocently looking from Nick to me, completely unaware of the bomb that was about to go off.

His demeanor changed when he noticed me silently crying, then his eyes shot to Nick.

Nicholas let out the breathe he'd been holding as he turned to face his best friend. "Why is she crying, Wesley?" he asked firmly.

Wesley gave me a stern look, one that I'd never seen before. It was resignation to the truth, to the fact that he too had been struggling with the lie.

"Look Nick, we never meant to hurt you. It just happened."

The statement brought bile up into my throat. I'd known it

was only a matter of time before the truth came out.

Nickolas took two swift steps towards Wesley and punched him square in the face. I watched as Wesley fell back a few steps and reached out to stop Nicholas from making contact a second time.

"You don't understand, "he tried to explain but Nicholas was walking past him and heading home.

I jumped out of my seat and followed behind Nick, thinking that maybe I could explain, say something to calm him down.

"Please Nicholas, let me explain," I called out, realizing that my words only managed to halt him completely and turn on me with the anger he had started taking out on Wesley.

"Explain?" he yelled, his face torn between anger and hurt. "Explain what exactly. That my best friend and my girl..." he trailed off not knowing exactly how to finish the sentence, probably realizing that he didn't even know what we had done.

"We made a mistake," I cried out, my hand covering my chest, trying to hold in the pain I was feeling not only emotionally but physically as well.

"A Mistake!" he returned, taking two steps closer. "What was the mistake? Tell me, please, so I can wrap my mind around how I can possibly understand this mistake."

I shook my head, not knowing how to admit to him that I'd

slept with his best friend in a drunken stupor.

Wesley put the palm of his hand on the base of my back, the heat stalling my movements.

"We had sex, Nick. We were drunk and you were in Atlanta looking for a job. We made a mistake, one we will never make again." He tried to explain but his words only forced Nicholas to charge at Wesley, pushing me out of the way.

He'd dropped him on the ground, his fist striking Wesley in the gut and side several times before Wesley could kick him off. Wesley rustled himself to his feet and jumped several feet away from Nicholas, holding his hand out, as if waving the white flag.

"We knew the moment we were done it was wrong." Wesley tried, but his words fell on deaf ears.

Nicholas got back on his feet and glared at me. "You..." he stood straighter, pointing his finger at me, "You're a whore who's ruined everything. I hope you rot in hell."

How words could cut sharper than a knife I couldn't say, but he'd done just that. He was right, I was and I had ruined everything.

He stormed past me, leaving me looking out into the street catching a pair of eyes I'd never expected to see. Papa Tom stood at the edge of his driveway, just at the main street, with his hand to his mouth and the look of shame in his eye.

I took in a breath, finally realizing what I had done, the devastation surrounding me. My grandfather stood unmoving as Wesley came to my side as I fell to the ground and sobbed uncontrollably.

"Let's go inside Mags, people are watching," he whispered into my hair, trying his best to get me to my feet.

I honestly can't remember what happened that afternoon, or that night. The following days were a blur as well, but mostly they were filled with Wesley by my side as I cried in and out of sleep, stuck in bed with the worse case of undisclosed morning sickness.

Abuelita finally came in to my room on the third morning after the big blow out and flat out asked me, "Margaret, are you pregnant?"

My eyes could only focus on her for a moment before I felt the nausea kick in, the room starting its slow spin. I leaned off the bed and barely made it in to the small garbage can next to my bed. I didn't need to answer, the reaction clear as day.

"Then it is Wesley's?" she asked, boldly.

Leaning back on my pillow, I made eye contact with her. "Yes," I managed to admit.

She began to nod, "I figured as much. Tom came over the other night, upset about what he had seen the other day. I tell you, I've never seen the old man so upset in all my life."

It didn't help that I was the youngest of all his grandchildren and I looked so much like my father, his son.

I cleared my throat and felt myself on the verge of tears. "I don't know what to do, Abuelita."

She leaned towards me and gave me a hug, her fragile body feeling so tender upon mine. "My precious child. You will do what you must," she said softly, a mist filling her eyes as well.

"They don't know. No one does," I admitted, worry filling me where fear once had.

Her lips pierced together as she stared down at me. "You need to tell them, Wesley at least. One way or another, the truth is bound to come out," an odd sadness sounded in her voice.

"I don't want Nicholas knowing, he can't, he will never forgive me, Abuelita. I love him."

Abuelita shushed me with a finger to my lips, "You need to rest, my love. We can work this out when you feel better. I will go make you something to settle your stomach." She got up without saying another word and left me there to think about Papa Tom and how disappointed in me he must feel.

I did what Abuelita suggested, I rested and spent a few days trying to get my bearing backs. Wesley came over once or twice but I didn't tell him why I was really sick. It was easier when he visited after his shift at work, I'd gotten past the difficult mornings and was somewhat normal.

By weeks' end, Tom finally showed up at Abuelita's door.

"Hi Papa," I said, opening the door for him.

"Margaret," he replied, coming in to the kitchen. "Is your grandmother here?" he asked.

"She is resting. Do you want me to go get her?" asking meant I would escape sitting down and having a chat of our own.

"No, I think you and me is how it will be this one time," he stated, pulling out a seat from the table and sitting down. Papa's eyes met mine and he reached a hand out, insinuating that I take a seat in front of him.

I found myself sitting, facing him, and staring into disappointed eyes. Not wanting to cry, I found eyes shifting to the table, to my hands that lay in front of me.

"So you and Nicholas are over," he began, waiting for me to answer. I nodded, which in turn forced a sigh to escape his mouth.

"Are you going to Brown or not, Margaret?" he asked plainly, getting right to the purpose of his visit.

My eyes shot to his, "I can't go." The words coming out without thinking that he would obviously want an explanation.

"You can't or you won't? I had to pull some major stings to have your application approved Margaret. This opportunity doesn't come every day, dear. In fact, it's a once in a lifetime opportunity," he scolded.

The truth of his words making me feel worse. I hadn't just ruined my relationship, but also my future.

"I can't. I'm pregnant," I said firmly, sitting up a little straighter. Feeling the freedom of saying it to someone else aside from Abuelita.

"What?" he shouted, getting up from his seat. His face turning 3 shades of crimson darker.

Abuelita came into the kitchen, just as his chair fell to the floor. "Why are you yelling?" her raised voice catching both of our attentions.

He turned to her, "this girl has gone and ruined her future, that's why I'm yelling."

She shook her head at him, "as if she is the first girl to go getting pregnant, Tom," she said calmly. "Dear Lord, you make it sound like her life is over."

"Consuela…" his hands went up, trying to get her to see reason.

"No, Tom. No," she started. "Tell me, do you love your granddaughter?" she asked him, boldly.

His spine straightened, and his body stiffened. "You know I

love her, that is not the point."

"No?"

"No, it's not."

"Then we will do everything we can to help her."

He turned to me and looked me over, finally nodding his head, understanding her meaning.

"Fine." He nodded more vigorously. "You have a choice to make young lady," he said gravely.

"You can stay here and lose me as your grandfather..." he said, taking a moment to look at Consuela who had shot her chin up in the air.

"Or you go to Brown....in the condition that you're in and never come back. I will take care of you and your baby, but you are to make a name for yourself. You are to become someone you want that child to look up to."

23 NO MATTER WHERE

June 2015

Maggie sat out on the front porch when all her cousins left that afternoon. She'd known the bomb she dropped on them would no doubt create a distance on her relationship with a few of them, especially Melanie, but she wouldn't feel bad about having an amazing daughter waiting for her back at home.

She removed her cell phone from her pocket and dialed Arden's number. Arden, her oldest and dearest friend had agreed to watch Olivia so that she could make this trip. He'd been sending her text messages daily since she'd arrived, she just hadn't voiced her feeling about missing Olivia to Devin or Consuela.

"Hi there, beautiful. I was wondering if you were going to call at some point," he chuckled into the line.

"How is my baby girl?" she sighed, feeling the tug in her chest.

"She is great, doesn't even realize that you're gone," he teased. The joke, while apparent made her wonder.

"I'm joking Maggie, she is right here, let me put her on the line," he said, the line going quiet before she could sass him.

"Hi mommy." Olivia's little voice burst through the line.

"Hi my sweet, how has Arden been treating you?" Maggie asked, curious what wonders Arden had concocted for her daughter.

"Oh, you know, his boyfriend Barry built me the most amazing blanket fort ever!" she squealed into her ear.

Maggie smiled, pleased that Arden hadn't made Barry stay away just because he was sitting Olivia.

"It can't be better than our magical fort," Maggie instigated, knowing their blanket fort had been pretty spectacular.

She giggled into the phone, "I don't know mommy, it really is amazing."

"Sweetie, I miss you so much," Maggie sighed into the line, her sadness coming through.

"Was it terribly sad, the funeral for great grandpa Tom?" she asked, her tender youth clearing her heart for the nice memories she'd shared with Tom.

"It was, my love, but I will be home before you know it. Put Arden back on the phone for me sweetie."

"I love you mommy," she said finally, waiting for Maggie to reply.

"I love you too baby," Maggie's face changed, knowing that no matter what, her daughter's voice could change any day into a good day.

"So when is your flight back?" he asked her as soon as he came back on the line.

"I was planning on coming back tomorrow. George wants me in his office first thing Monday morning, and I don't see any way around it," I admitted, making it clear that life moves on from my current location.

"Well, send me a text when you board your plane and we will have your welcome home banner up and ready for you."

"Thank you Arden. I will talk to you soon."

Clicking the phone she didn't realize that Nicholas had walked all the way up to the porch and was leaning against the post at the far end. He was watching her as she talked to her daughter. The change in her appearance was remarkable. He'd never seen her so relaxed, genuine, in his whole time with her.

He cleared his throat and found that he'd startled her. Not being able to contain himself, he laughed at the reaction.

She'd almost come out of her seat.

"Damn it, Nick," she gasped, "you scared the shit out of me."

"You know I didn't mean to scare you," he started, making his way to sit in the chair next to her.

"How long were you standing there?" she asked him curiously.

A smile spread across his face, "long enough to notice how you light up when you talk to Olivia," his eyes sparkled when he mentioned the little girl.

"She is my world, Nick," Maggie admitted clearly, finally feeling the freedom to talk about her daughter without fear of hurting anyone's feeling.

"You ready for that dinner you promised me?"

She sat back, and looked at him fully, taking in the way the light of the sun caught in his brown hair, and how his skin gleamed a bronze she'd only known models to wear.

"Tell me something, honestly."

"Anything," he replied, waiting for the other shoe to drop.

"Could you live your life with me, love me, knowing that Olivia is your best friend's daughter?" It was a question Maggie had always known she would ask if ever given the opportunity to have a second chance with him.

He took in a breath, mostly because he'd had 7 years to contemplate the answer to this very question. He'd gone over it in his mind so many times that he shook his head at her. "Maggie, I've loved you from the very moment I laid eyes on you sitting on this very porch watching us play stick ball the day you came to live here. I've loved you my whole life. I've loved you through the most hurtful moments of our lives, but they hurt because I knew that even then, when you'd gone and done the unthinkable, I wouldn't be able to stop loving you." His eyes welled with tears and hers began to mirror his.

"I said some pretty terrible things to you, but they came from a hurt I'd not known was possible to feel. Maggie, I forgave you the moment I saw you in the park 7 years ago. I was just too much of a coward to come out and admit it to myself, or to you."

She jumped out of her seat and jumped into his arms, "Oh, Nicholas!" Her arms wrapped around his neck, her lips pressing firmly onto his.

Time stood still for the two of them. Their life had come full circle on that porch. From the first time they saw each other, to moments of waiting, to hearts breaking and to now finally accepting the love that had never died between them.

Pulling back, she looked him in the eyes, "I have to go home tomorrow," admitting sadly.

"What are your thoughts about that?" he asked her, giving

her the liberty to stake the claims of their new relationship, because a relationship there would be.

Wondering herself how things would work, she was more concerned how Olivia would take having a new man come in to her life. She had such a strange relationship with Wesley, she didn't know how Olivia would feel about Nicholas.

"I think it will depend on Livy," Maggie admitted truthfully, knowing that her daughter was the most important person in her life.

"Maggie, I'm with you no matter where we end up. If it means I move to Chicago, then so be it, but I'm not letting you go this time," he said, his arms squeezing a little tighter around her waist.

Nodding softly, she laid her head on his shoulder, "I can't imagine how we survived 10 years apart," she whispered sheepishly.

He agreed, looking back and feeling as though life had never been complete without her.

Nicholas saw the figure walking towards them before Maggie did. He felt Wesley staring them down, feeling the outsider as he reached the porch.

When the muscles on Nicholas began to tense up, Maggie realized something was up. She sat up and found Nick staring at something behind her. Turning she found Wesley smiling at her.

"I come in peace," he said, his hands going up in response.

Maggie chuckled at his parley, and how silly he looked. "We accept your peace and return the white flag," she mused at him, praying Nicholas would concede.

"Want to go out to a goodbye dinner with us?" he surprised the two of them. Wesley nodded, his face erupting in a cheerfulness missing from his face for some time.

"Yeah, man. Thanks, that sounds nice. Now all we need is Melanie," he added pulling out his cell phone.

Maggie stopped him, "Wes, I told her everything this afternoon. She may not be ready to join the festivities."

He registered what she was saying but inwardly wondered how she felt. She'd known bits and pieces of the story for so long and now after all this time, the truth was set ablaze.

"Let me call her anyway. Maybe she will be up for it," he tried, walking away for a moment to make the attempt.

Nicholas and Maggie watched him in the distance, seeing as he paced back and forth on the driveway as he talked to her in a hushed voice. Finally he ended the call and walked back over to them.

"Yeah, she isn't ready, but I'm sure she will come around. You mean so much to her, Mags. And hey, if Nick and I can patch things up, I'm sure Melanie has it in her," he said.

They went out to dinner, the three of them, that night and celebrated old friends and a love that never died. Maggie slept in Nicholas' arms one final time before she had to leave him.

In the middle of the night she woke up and walked outside to sit in the moonlight at the base of his driveway. She'd spent so many moonlight nights praying that she would find herself in that very moment. Happy and in love again, the only difference was that she had never imagined that it would be with Nicholas again.

He had felt her stir and leave his side. He'd let her walk out of the room and out of the house without stopping her. Saw how she sat on the ground and wondered what was going on in her beautiful mind.

He only went to her side when he realized that she was crying. It took everything in him not to run.

Sitting next to her, he wrapped an arm around her waist. "What's going on Magpie, why are you crying?"

Without looking at him, she laid her head on his shoulder, "I finally have what I've been writing about for so many years. I finally have the love my heart has been aching for since I left Carmen Street all those years ago."

He placed a kiss on her forehead, "I guess happily ever after isn't just something in books, is it?"

April Gutierrez

ABOUT THE AUTHOR

April Gutierrez's passion for writing began as a young girl and it continues still today. She has written several books in different genres and wants to pursue as many genres as is possible.

April lives in Florida with her husband and three beautiful children. Besides writing, she loves theater and vintage movies.

www.ingramcontent.com/pod-product-compliance
Lightning Source LLC
Chambersburg PA
CBHW070818120626
46556CB00002B/563